My name is Jomo Sekou Henderson. All my life There was absolutely nothing that I obtained that did not exact a price. Nothing was simple, nor was it easy. Starting from my birth. Born as a premature baby. My Birth Certificate didn't even list my weight it was so unbelievably low. The hospital demanded that my Mother sign almost a full ream of documents absolving them of their liabilities in the event of my imminent demise (as they believed it to be) before I was to be released into her care. From my first days alive There were people counting on my death, negotiating on how to rid themselves of responsibility in its details. I could not have known these things at the time, but they would soon become the forecasting of many patterns of events to come. I dealt with and ultimately conquered bouts of aggressing parental rearing, abandonment, and neglect. There was psychological abuse within my own home before I reached the age of nine, or even able to even know or realize. Had it not been my Grandmother who instilled in me just enough support and reinforcement for me to become self-reliant (before I fully understood what that even meant). That and the upbringing delivered from two very different yet extremely similar individuals in matters regarding being mental militancy. What they created was a formidable mind and a resilient young man who to this day can only be described by those who actually know me enough personally as relentless. While still quite green in many other areas, I had no other choice but to figure out most of everything else on my own. This dis-advantage/ vantage point (perspective) merely forged me into an active listener, and keen observant to behaviors many would not pick up. After working several jobs, by mostly talking myself into the front door without taking "No" for an answer, much was learned about employment and life. So much so that I took initial steps into entrepreneurial ventures not enthused in being an employee longer than need be.

SHAPING
OF AN AGENT

By

JOMO SEKOU HENDERSON

Paperback: 978-1-7321438-4-5
Hardcover: 978-0-578-24712-0
Hardcover [LTD Ed]: 978-0-578-24713-7
E-book: 978-1-63848-513-1
Audiobook: TBA
Library of Congress Number: TBA
First Paperback Edition: March 2021.

Edited by Shernece Roberts & Jomo Sekou Henderson
Cover art by Shernece Roberts, Sheeba Maya,
Layout by Shernece Roberts & Jomo Henderson
Photographs' by Markay Mason

Printed by LULU in the U.S.A.
TVPC Agency(dba)[Publisher]
703 Bullard Manor
Whiteman AFB, Missouri 6530

DEDICATION

Preface:

I believe this: That there are only a few 'personalities' that exist. There are randomized reconfigurations amongst the people who populate this world. That's why some of us look alike, act similarly, think similarly. This is why we resonate with people altogether. These people we resonate with remind us of others we have known personally before. We hope for rebirthed, comparative associations with these people. I also take this belief into how I see this world and its inhabitants...We are all members of one neighborhood. When you seek to find an audience, you first must understand where "you" fit into that assortment of personalities in "that" neighborhood. Fitting in the sense of knowing oneself, and what that means to you as a person. Understanding oneself enough to know what those unique differences are. Never altering oneself 'to' fit in...

My Dedication:

I dedicate this book to all the truly caring and integral personalities within this universe that align with mine. I dedicate this book to anyone that has lived and experienced much, who have not given up on their goals or given up on searching for them, fighting for them, and doing their very best to develop them into better ones until successful completion has been brought into Fruition. I especially dedicate this to younger versions of myself left to figure out a great many things on their own and not even know in the start which way is up. Keep pushing.

Thank you to my Lord and Savior, Jesus Christ for mixing into the ingredients that created me all that was included.

CONTENTS

Acknowledgments

I want to acknowledge my Father, Laverne M. Henderson, and my Mother, Madelyn V. Ward. May you both rest in heavenly peace. I love you both, and I always will. I need to Acknowledge my phenomenal Wife, Alecia Henderson, and my amazing Son, Marcellus Sekou Henderson. You have given me what I searched many years for. A family of my own. Thank you! For the support the peace and our ongoing collective growth as a family!

There were Women that came into my life that for the most part forever altered my trajectory in just about every imaginable way; intellectually, emotionally, and spiritually. These Women are in order of appearance; Mayme Dunbar, Izetta Henderson-Boone, Virginia Moore, Marjory Moore, Dorothy Jackson-Brown, Cynthia Bowie-Coleman, Judith Ward, and Louise Johnson. I thank you all, some of you I continue to pray for as you have crossed over to the other side of this life. The ones who remain with I pray for your well-being continuously.

There were Several OG's who took the time to teach a young, angry, stubborn, and hard headed youth with potential a great many things... Some good, and some not as good. All appreciated, to all of which I shall remain grateful. These Men are in order of appearance; Calvin Henderson, Mark Henderson, George Steele, David Ward, Frank Myers Jr., Otis Scruse, Alonzo Davis, Curtis Bell, James "Chuck" Brown, Jimmy "Speedy" Harden, Ben "Uncle Ben" Pernell, Rodney Morrison, Frank Palisano, Keith Norman, and Ross Chandler. I thank you all, I continue to pray for you all here and passed on. What you have given me individually and collectively is appreciated and cherished beyond any know form of measurement.

To my lifelong friends; naming these people in order of their appearance; Raymond Brown, William Mason, Raymond, Robert, & Richard Parker/Hackett, Eddie Rogers, Fatin Bell, James McCray, Alex Mobley, David Petro, Charlie Mackie, Frank Myers the 3rd, Rashaan Pugh, Maurice Pugh, Eddie Moore, Capricia Moore, John & Chris Moore, Theodore "Super Chuck" Miles, Jeffery Miller, LaPaul Phelps, Orlando Mclean, Derek Golson, Lance Hunt, Harold Mercedes, Stanley Shields, Kevin Anderson, and Quinton Whitaker.

Annabelle Steele, Tikka Steele, Patricia Steele, Jerome Steele, Kenneth Steele, Every part of Amityville, Wyandanch, the Poospatuck Indian Reservation, South-Side Jamaica Queens, The entire Bronx, Brooklyn, Harlem, Buffalo, Iroquois Job Corps Crew, and Alumni! All my Miami and Key West extended Family, and all my Atlanta extended Family! All my Starke, Orange Park, and Jacksonville Extended Family! Duuuval!

CHAPTER I

"Double Deal"

Students milled about the halls of Eastern high, casually calling out to each other as they passed in the bright florescent corridors of their school; blissfully unaware of the unsanctioned activity happening amid them all. One student in particular; went about his business unbothered by the consequences of getting caught, still taking time to greet those calling out to him; after-all, he was confident he wouldn't.

Taylor's innate ability to discern a change in even the smallest of details made him aware of the trickery about to take place. Stopping in his tracks, insulted by the slight, Taylor addressed his client and longtime friend; Student life still flowing steadily around the pair, like a stream would around a blockage.

"Hey man. What's this?"

The young man's shoulder touched the crook of his neck. Shrugging as he responded to Taylor.

"What you mean?"

"Look, I got shit to do! You're fucking with my time and I don't appreciate that shit." Taylor's tone increasingly aggravated as he continued. "Give me what the fuck we agreed upon yo!"

Conceding defeat, the kid's short arms waves in surrender.

"Ok! Ok, damn kid, don't get testy. I was just fuckin with ya."

"Do I look like a fucking toy to you?" Taylor questioned, his voice raising even louder in volume.

The crew rolling with him paid close attention to Taylor's demeanor, realizing that he might make an aggressive move on the guy; a silent tension building slowly in the moments that followed, each member of his team on high alert, waiting for what happens next.

"Cough up the money dummy!"

He reaches for the rest of the cash, walking towards Taylor trying to make light of it all...

"Ok, I see you don't have a sense of humor." Discretely handing the balance over, he ends his surrender with a last remark.

"No problem Taylor, here you go. We straight now?"

Leaning forward before he let's go, Taylor whispers in his ear. "You're getting way too comfortable being disrespectful to me. If I were you - I wouldn't do that again. We've been cool for a lot of years now, you've never had to see me when I ain't in a pleasant mood and you don't want none of this smoke I have for those who take my kindness for weakness. Don't play with my money again. I won't say it again either!"

Mostly, Taylor showed himself as astute, all while being methodically gregarious when dealing with his peers. It was only on rare occasions that he had to shed that easy going demeanor before making an unfortunate example out of one of his schoolmates. Inconspicuously tending to his business, Taylor would supply his classmates with items they wanted, yet would not easily have access to under normal circumstances. Even in the ninth grade there were brief moments where he schemed to gain information, before seizing each opportunity afforded to him to find himself in the right place at the right time. Taking advantage of each opportunity, Taylor had to accommodate exclusive clients, deviating from normal routes to separate himself from his peers. Navigating fluidly between activities, whilst ensuring the integrity of his actions always kept the more discrete exchanges between the prestigious elite upperclassmen and select members of the faculty confidential.

A typical day for Taylor, at least until the bell rang.

As many of his classmates scattered to their respective classes, Taylor and his team would occasionally go elsewhere. The group fashioned themselves as all-stars in their own rights despite their freshman status, ahead of their time, and at their ages they were well aware of this; even going with their own mantra, 'The cream just rose to the top.'

For many related and unrelated reasons, Taylor was becoming increasingly known within the school for several things - One of them being his growing business, and the other, his appetite for more clients and influence.

"Hey let's go." Taylor said to his crew.

Clearing the rear fence to the campus with a little help from a few of the truancy specialists.

Vaughn unlike Taylor remained aware of the many things happening around him. As the eldest cousin, also well known for many reasons- some because of circumstances stemming from incidents that had taken place at the school and back in the neighborhood. Overall, he was a respected junior earning his place among the far upper echelon of masculinity at the High School without challenge. However, he increasingly frustrated with what he had been noticing with his cousin's sudden loss in interest for his academic responsibilities. See, Vaughn knew fully well that their Uncle would not find Taylor's deviations satisfactory.

Unaware that his cousin always made sure his crew either did their assignments on time or had a group of wannabes associated with his crew look over what they could get done, even finishing it sometimes, or assist his friends in completing their assignments altogether.

Taylor had also begun arrangements with certain teachers and administrative staff dealing with attendance; having them occasionally doctor their reports. The work was being done, and their attendance was basically a non-issue at this point; until they took their campaign beyond the schools' walls, where the board game shifted beyond Taylor's manipulative grasp and the expanding sphere of growing influence.

Although he was unaware of just how far his Uncle Demetrius's influence was in the community, Taylor surely was creating the opportunity for his awakening to this sobering reality.

As the group enjoyed their momentary escape, a single pair of eyes spotted them. Making a call, setting the day's key events in motion.

Vaughn had been uneasy as he sat in his mid-day study hall class. He already knew the inevitable was coming, and Mr. Inevitable himself was standing in the doorway holding his visitors' pass, gesturing for Vaughn to join him in the hallway. Vaughn sighed, leaning into the chair. His back stiffens as he crosses his legs, placing the right over his left thigh, staring respectively at his Uncle. His look contrite yet hoping at the same time his uncle understood he simply had no answers. It took a moment for him to muster up the energy needed to stand erect and face this head on, joining his uncle in the hallway.

"How have your classes been treating you so far, Vaughn?"

"Uncle Demetrius, what do you honestly expect me to do?"

"So, you're finding yourself in a difficult position? The bond you both shared for all this time is changing right before your very eyes. I can understand how this must feel, as it also explains why I didn't find out from you." Shifting his hands into the pockets of his perfectly tailored dress pants, he continued.

"What I find... more complex is how you're in class and your younger cousin is not. This is an issue for me. If you cannot monitor or even influence this expectation, we once thought manageable, then I will find another method that will." Vaughn understood that any additional remark would not be in his overall favor; reassuring his Uncle he would take a more direct role in getting his cousin to realize, again. This time his methods would prove effective.

Demetrius stood still momentarily, shifting slightly the placement of his hands as he listens to his nephew. Placing his right hand on his nephew's shoulder, looking into his eyes before declaring that I would handle the situation; granting him a warm smile before allowing Vaughn to get back to his studies.

Newly motivated, Demetrius departs the school, heading to rejoin his modest escort detail, waiting with his entourage in tow. An unknown part of his strategy forming with each step, for the plan to get his young nephew exactly where he wanted him to be.

A few miles away from the school, Taylor stepped out of the corner store, a beverage in his left hand and a newspaper in the other. His eyes squinting slightly against the glare of the morning sun, exhaling in contemplation, taking a moment to savor the distinct aromas of the city; marveling at the energy of the everyday people and the busyness that came with living life; the hum of the city a symphony in his ears, as Taylor's eyes closed, becoming totally enveloped by the orchestral sounds of horns honking, people chattering, and rhythmic thuds of footsteps hitting the pavement, drumming the very beats that made the bustling sounds of a community come to life.

Clutching his paper, Taylor made his way through Poot and Ox, heading towards an unoccupied park bench nearby. Spunk and Geno headed towards the alleyway near the corner store - even though they were out of plain view, you could still hear them laughing faintly; and though at this distance, he could still tell his boys were around, probably playing with the dice they had a habit of carrying around, just waiting for opportunities like this. Feeling somewhat accomplished in his developing skill sets, and the ability to coordinate the activities of many around him without garnishing much attention from what he could detect, anyway; Taylor mused at the little success. Four pages deep into his paper, with over twenty minutes to spare before they were due back at school, he heard an eerily familiar sound.

He stilled. His paper forgotten as he listened most attentively. He had grown to know the distinct sound of new tires moving in unison, going at the same speed methodically, with one unanimous mission. His brows creased at the realization that he was in the direct path of his uncle's motorcade, and he swore. Demetrius had not a concern in the world amongst the armed security, once he made eye contact with his nephew sitting on the park bench table, looking on at him in respectful amusement as he approached. He smiled.

Upon his arrival the two men briefly embraced with sincere blissful sentiment. It did not take long for that moment to pass before Demetrius spoke, acting as if there was very little time to spare, and each moment was crucial to some eminent importance.

"I have been observing you, Young Taylor. Seems we have quite a few mutual acquaintances in the city, and I've come across some interesting information how these people knew my nephew."

Taylor clenched his jaw, relaxing his mouth and releasing pressure from his teeth as he realized his discernment had not failed him; and that sound was indeed his Uncle Demetrius and his team. Not what he had wanted for sure, especially while he was still basking in his tactical intelligence just moments prior. With few other options to go with, Taylor smirked with a bashfully yet menacing expression and responded calmly.

"I really wished that you had waited for just about five more minutes before you rolled up, I was almost content with my accomplishments this morning."

"Oh well, too bad I ruined that moment of self-actualization you were having, what exactly had you come to realize again?" Demetrius responded, folding his hands while he spoke. "Apparently, I do not know the full extent of what you're even celebrating. However, what I know is that you are a bit cavalier in your execution. This much I know for certain. I think your self-actualization needs some re-evaluation young man. Find your way back in the same way or preferably a better way than you got out and take my advice; Leave these trips for after you're released."

Pensively, Taylor watches as his uncle stands up from his rested position on the bench, walking away.

He spoke again before entering the rear driver's side door of his vehicle, "Be mindful young Taylor, although it may seem like it, your time is not necessarily your own to waste."

Even though Taylor had heard his Uncle speaking to him in his distinct corrective tone for years, this sentiment did not seem of the usual variety. He was now curious and determined to make sense of yet another journey set before him by his Uncle, who never seemed to disappoint with his mystery.

CHAPTER 2

"Formation"

No longer enticed by the contents of his paper, placing it at his side to pass it off earlier than he normally would to one of his partners. For a few moments, Taylor sat stewing over what could have possibly been the purpose behind his Uncle's words, after all he never spoke without a deliberate motive.

He was the sole definition of what being methodical personified appeared to be. A mixture between bewilderment and anticipation keeping him in a stupor; until a sharp, but melodic horn blew- startling him back into awareness.

His maternal Uncle Khaleel was riding through the areas he usually would have been.

"Hey Nephew! What's your ass doing out here? We both know that you're supposed to be in that school," He hollered; Waving his hands backwards, gesturing towards the direction of the school behind them both "I'm shocked that Demetrius hasn't found you

yet."

Taylor's facial expression revealed his embarrassment because this had already taken place, moreover to the obvious awkwardness in seeing how apparently everyone but him saw this probable eventuality occurring as well. Taylor took a moment to deliver his retort.

"I see that you're funny in the morning too, Unc. Now you both got me over here really wondering if I have some type of tracking chip or something," A slow smile forming as he continued. "I wouldn't put it past either of you for real."

Khaleel smirked at Taylor's comment before he responded.

"It's too early for that. What would he need to chip you for? We're at home nephew... How many times do I need to remind you that nothing, absolutely nothing happens around here without one of us, meaning all of us won't know almost immediately?" Khaleel chuckled as he addressed his nephew.

"I thought you were catching on, but I can see that even though you're making some growths, you're still not seeing what's being shown. You need to get back to work, you're on the clock, T."

Khaleel left at the same speed he pulled up with and was back to whatever business he needed to attend to. A second visit in no less than five minutes had totally distracted Taylor from his morning escape, completely consumed by the inevitable discussion that was bound to happen at some point that evening. Taylor regrouped with his team, slipping in as stealthily as they slipped out, rewarding those who aided their re-entry appropriately.

Once back on the school compound, the group disbanded, going their separate ways, continuing the school day as planned.

Taylor found himself keen, willing the clock forward to end the period of waiting; anticipation of the weighted conversation with his uncle swimming in his head, and he was ready for it to be over with, relieving himself of this uncomfortable tension.

With his Uncle being the Delegate for DC, a unique position; He was unlike any other member of Washington's electoral body. Often, there would be a certain guest at the house for dinner, and Taylor usually had an active role that night.

With a Father often away on active-duty assignment, the son and nephew of two highly decorated veterans in their own respects had bragged on and spoke highly of- expected that when these dinner guests would come to visit, their evening also include the introduction and further acquaintance of the frequently regarded host.

This also was a process to usher in his own name's sake for when that time would come, for him to endeavor into his own official maneuvers he would make his name known to those who make most things happen.

Again, Demetrius was a most methodical individual indeed.

That evening Demetrius had his catering staff arrange the seating area of the dining room like they normally would have. With a touch of fastidiousness, he maneuvered throughout the reception areas of the home multitasking for the remaining hour/ after business calls, checking his appearance, their home and the progress of the catering staff during their preparation in the kitchen.

Taylor often envisioned his uncle running some prestigious restaurant in the same fashion; whilst the familiar smells of cinnamon and melting brown sugar filled the air with its powerful aroma.

Taylor could tell by the spices permeating the air and assaulting his olfactory senses with a pleasant surprise of apple pie. His absolute favorite, paired with the savory scents of floral

and pine as meats seasoned to perfection with rosemary and various other spices, were being seared and sauteed currently by the catering staff a few feet away.

The evening went on as a cavalcade of vehicles lined the driveway, each guest disembarking from the stream of jetblack SUVs. Walking a path, they have become so familiar with.

Laughter filled the concrete pavement leading directly to the entryway of the house as guests greeted each other, happy to be away from the formality of their respective positions of power.

Demetrius easily orchestrated these events that brought about the cheerful side of everyone; even some of the dreariest individuals in his circle. This is what he did well, amongst his many other skills and talents in interpersonal interactions. After approximately forty-five minutes of entertaining in the outer living room, the dining area then opened. They introduced his guests to the dining room with moderate showmanship.

Shrill sounds of metal hitting the crystal water goblet commanded the attention of each guest. Demetrius' authoritative demeanor casting a shadow of omnipotence as he welcomed his guests into his home, thanking them for enhancing the status of his evening dinner.

For Demetrius, these dinners were truly at the heart of his home. Each person would enter a stranger and by night's end leave feeling like a connected member of the family.

A quintessential element used to forge these bonds was laughter, helping them navigate through riveting discussions on a litany of subject matters, serious in context while becoming jovial and relaxed. This is what Demetrius represented.

A habitual display of transparency, giving him the ability to wield the power of persuasion without deceiving. At least not intentionally anyway. Few found the will to say no to an individual who moved in this fashion. He was certainly a no holds barred kind of guy. This was a large part of his effectiveness as a political figure overall. From his left to his right, he introduced:

"First, we have someone who most of you have heard of, or possibly even had the pleasure and privilege of watching on the court here in town when he led our team to two championships... a frequent guest here, the incomparable, Jaedon Newsome!"

"Next one of my distinguished colleagues from across the aisle; a true patriot and visionary for not only her constituents in New York but for us all as Americans, congressional representative from New York, Melissa Hohfrum."

"Next is one of my friends here in D.C. who once was a frequent visitor here in these halls, Associate Dean of academics with Howard University's School of Business, Tymieka Delson."

"I'd also like to humbly introduce my esteemed brother Denard's only Son Taylor. He is the pride of us both. Taylor is fifteen, turning sixteen, and these are the murky and conflicting years of his teens as we can all surely emphasize with." Demetrius says, smiling warmly at his nephew before he continues. "The group of fine professionals who keep my nephew and I, and the occasional return of my brother well nourished, and in need of physical training, meticulously trained and managed by a childhood friend of mine.

Surely a most trusted partner in most of how I can be the multitasker you know me to be. Our parents also grew up close with one another; raised basically as brothers. It is with supreme delight I present to you the culinary impresario Paolito Evensa!"

The group got down to the pressing matters of eating, drinking and enjoying one another's company after the introductions had concluded; Demetrius taking special delight in the careful curation of dinner guests whenever workable, offering an evening where people, who under normal circumstances would not usually have access to one another, because of a host of societal limitations.

This also was to the benefit of Taylor. Demetrius brought these hand-picked groups into their home to further stress his overall development.

Taylor was told that they would soon give the application submitted its due diligence.

Listening to his Uncle and congressional representative Hohfrum debate several political viewpoints, more on a few pieces of legislature that each had been working through their respective processes.

Jaedon spent many an afternoon showing Taylor how to play basketball, and how to train his body to perform at a high level, since Taylor had his first memories of training. He enjoyed when Jaedon came by. It was a good evening filled with an endless supply of group, side conversations, and side group conversations.

It was growing late, and the shuttle service drivers were pulling into the front area of our grand home. Prompting the guests to file out into the elevator, their departure faintly heard from the terrace as sounds of laughing, and voices speaking drifted into the night air declaring their enjoyment of the lingering moments of the evening's events.

Taylor took a few moments to gaze upon the departure of guest as they exited the side entrance of their lavish home, before getting into their chauffeured SUV's. Quite a few thoughts ran through his mind as he stood there looking on. Somehow, he always seemed astonished by the disparity in the way many of the people's life exposed him to as he experienced life.

He had seen many nights like this one, filled with opulent laughter, bursting with enjoyment; being apart from seeing others find happiness and peace as they vividly discuss the apparent and impactful despairs experienced all over the world.

This was always something that stimulated to him, capturing his attention as he marinated in those thoughts. His Uncle also making his way out, stood alongside him on the terrace.

For a moment Demetrius wanted to make a

point, hesitating briefly before finally announcing his entrance, as he observed his nephew with endearment. His weary eyes watched in the same manner, gazing at young Taylor with the same look he had been wearing just moments prior.

Realizing that his nephew was no longer a young child and quickly proving that he was growing into quite an ingenious young man. Reluctantly, he considered how deceptive time appeared to be; simply flying by, while simultaneously trying to deceive his own self of where it went.

A feeble attempt to disregard the tragic events of how he lost his sister-in-law Dorothy- Taylor's mother, her sister Della, and her husband Isaac, who tried his best to defend them both, but was just outnumbered and outgunned.

Not Taylor, his father Denard, nor Demetrius himself had truly made many attempts to deal with the circumstances of that disastrous evening, roughly nine years ago. Forced to collect himself, Demetrius' mind comes back to the present, remembering that coincidentally enough, its anniversary was just a few weeks away.

Their small group had surely grown closer as a family in the face of many challenges after losing Dorothy, Della, and Isaac; All murdered, trying to assassinate Denard. A poorly planned venture, for he was not due to return home until a few days after the killings had occurred on September 14th, 2001.

Both men stood on the spacious terrace, Taylor still unaware his Uncle had been standing behind him, his eyes closed as he enjoyed the lingering scents of the robust feast they indulged in several hours before. Fighting against the dry smell of a summer's evening and the sterile sting of cleaning solutions as the staff and cleaning crew cleared the aftermath with efficiency.

Demetrius knew he was working with less time than he would have preferred to get his nephew ready for what was potentially becoming a genuine challenge, and a test of his character in the next few years. Possibly even losing him forever, if not carefully avoided.

No one person could have predicted an absolute outcome, how this dilemma was going to play itself out. The discussion of how Dorothy had passed never fully taken on- the deaths were so abrupt and devastating to the entire family and the community as well; driving tension even higher following the wake of 9/11 a few weeks earlier. What made the matter even that much more difficult had been that Vaughn, Taylor and Langston, Vaughn's younger brother, were there when it happened and could live after being threatened to follow their loved ones at gunpoint.

Even at the tender age of eight, Vaughn stood tall in front of Taylor, and Langston who had only been four years old in their pajamas staring down these full-grown men, as they watched their mothers' brutally beaten and shot after, like the young man his father had raised him to be.

The sight of Isaac being shot directly to the face and more times to his lifeless body, just for doing everything in how power to protect them all during the home invasion.

Demetrius approached Taylor finally, gently placing his palm on his right shoulder with a simple greeting.

"Hey Nephew"

Turning his head, Taylor looks around, his lips twisting into his signature half smirk as he grinned. His usual charm in place as he smiled up at his uncle.

"Hey Unc, how did you think the evening went?"

Demetrius's mulls, the familiar stoic mask still in place as he redirected the question back to his nephew.

"More important than that T, from your perspective, how was your experience? You already know my delight is to listen to and learn."

Not at all surprised by his uncle's response, this was usually his question to Taylor at this time of the evening - but more so, serving as a reminder that for the first time in a while, he wondered about that difficult, hardening period eight years ago when he lost his family.

Those thoughts led him to thinking about Vaughn and Langston, who lost both of their parents- while he still had a father of his own.

Taylor's face contorted as his lips twisted, curiosity peaking as he told his uncle about his night.

"I wasn't able to work the entire room because I spent much of my time speaking with Dean Delsn about my application process to Howard, but I got to clown some with Jaedon for a few moments."

Demetrius then steered the conversation to the events of earlier that day.

"No lecture."

This surprised Taylor as he listened to his uncle's reminder that conversation with Dean Delsn won't equate to much, if choices like leaving the property during school hours are events he planned to repeat.

Demetrius continued briskly reminding his nephew how his influence is without comparison in the area. He would not follow him, nor invade his privacy, but he need not put him in the position where he needed to watch him at the same time.

Taking a moment to let what he said on sink into Taylor's awareness, Demetrius concluded young Taylor had indeed received the messaged; and nodded in agreement, as they did many times before on other subjects, as Demetrius placed his hand softly on the side top part of his faded, wavy hair before turning around and leaving the terrace tending to his duties as master of his home. He watched on and waved farewells to the catering crew while they had wrapped up their duties, and one by one retired to their respective homes for the night.

Ever so quietly from the shadowy background inside the unit Taylor could hear his Uncle tell him "Good Evening" before he responded in kind, heading to his room

CHAPTER 3

"Seeded"

A few months before his graduation from Howard University, Taylor had become nothing less than a pure machine of commerce and service; Langston mostly was always around Taylor, but he along with his team - which started with roughly just four of them, sometimes seven kids when Vaughn and Langston were with there, grew that comradery into a real team. Overseeing many entrepreneurial ventures across the south and east side of the city. The most fascinating thing was their way of handling business. They always seemed to know who wanted what and executed that desire with such creative tactics; like a concierge would do, yet more effectively and always within a brief window of time.

Piling up owed favors along the way, Taylor collected handsome handling fees on both sides of the transaction. Their abilities to supply with the highest satisfaction had given them quite a unique status. One completely separating them from anyone else. From the right price for the coveted vehicle, to the forgotten diamond you needed for that anniversary you didn't remember until the day of.

Discretion was a strict requirement or he could easily face service banishment, amongst a host of other tools inspiring deterrence.

Taylor became masterful in finding the desired or needed by those better suited to meet his premiums. With the influence gained in the strategic transactions of opportunity, Taylor surely amassed influence on his own; along with the insight and wisdom in how to wield it.

Demetrius had been well aware of these developing situations since its inception and allowed them to progress. He knew his nephew enough to know that whatever he had created is used discreetly with some community benefit at its core. That is mainly who Taylor was, truly his Mother's son, whether he'd ever be aware of it or not. How could he? He was only six when she was taken from him.

A highly decorated student, Taylor was one of the co-captains on his Basketball team as well. Sharing the honor with a prospect that has been slated to enter the draft being projected to go 3rd overall. Taylor was approached early about the NBA route, but he softly declined to do so. Basketball had always been enjoyable for him and his friends. One of Jaedon's many prosperous proteges had become the coach for the Bison's around the time Taylor had entered the eleventh grade, after he himself blew out one of his knees playing ball overseas in the hopes of eventually making the league back in the states. Because of the relationship that he and

Jaedon shared. It transcended into the two of them beneficially for Taylor, except for his expectations, for his unrelenting tenacity on his court. The season provided Taylor with many opportunities to visit other communities around the country and exchange contacts and services for more than a few people high and low. He made the situation stretch his reach out far and effectively widespread. Both Denard, Demetrius, and Khaleel were very impressed. Those old enough, and native to the area long enough, attributed his prowess in areas of relatability, and interpersonal effectiveness to that of his late mother.

She too in her much different way seemed to also have an everreaching skill-set in embracing the hearts of many of the people whom she dealt with. Their approaches differed regarding the cornerstone of their motivations. Taylor's mother had been more philanthropic than entrepreneurial. It was actually the success of his mother in her dealings that laid the seed to the rise of the Fortune Family.

Born Dorothy Proffit, sister to over seven other siblings, most of which now live out of the area. Three still lived in the old neighborhood. The three that remained besides Dorothy were Della and Dwight, who is now better known as Khaleel. Dorothy had started out providing food for struggling families and using her influential networking skills to find employers who needed employees for their fledgling or freshly started business ventures. She continued to wedge herself during finding the things that those in her community, and others like it needed while having a knack of locating those who needed the skill-sets of those same community residents who she called her neighbors. Dorothy repeated connecting needs until her name meant more to these communities than any politician before her.

So, when she fell in love with the dashing Denard Fortune, she was ecstatic. During those years Denard had just come back to town from his third tour in Iraq and was always working in the community with various construction projects when he wasn't playing basketball between whichever park had the talent that day the strongest. He was actually the man who taught Jaedon how to play from the time he was about six himself. Denard had a marvelous way with words and equally effective with people, especially women. Denard had fun with these advantages until he and Dorothy grew closer than friends. Then her simplicity and sincerity struck him. Denard was twenty-eight when Dorothy became pregnant with Taylor. To build something larger from them all, Denard took an assignment that required a clearance he'd yet to need. This assignment partnered him with a few politicians from Capitol Hill and required him to make several deployments overseas during the initial phases of her pregnancy. It wasn't easy without question for Dorothy, but she did not have a thorough understanding of what failure felt like, so she persevered through those struggles. Denard could make it back to the neighborhood two days before Taylor was born. He stayed stateside for the next year, working more closely on Capitol Hill.

His younger brother Demetrius had himself just graduated early from Howard University himself and joined the Airforce as an Officer where they put him into the areas of Intelligence. He served four years per his contract, then ran for the delegate's seat for the District. With Denard and

Dorothy being the couple they had been, and Demetrius having had just recently served, Dorothy's influence literally ushered him into office. They worked closely to enhance the quality of life for those in the community, and their own family in a stunningly short amount of time. Demetrius methodically bought the Chestnut building shortly thereafter, and a few other choice properties in the area in a short period after that as their initiative to revitalize the community around those properties also experienced much success for all involved. between the two of them they found new and unconventional ways to allocate resources to renovate and revamp the entire southside with plans to duplicate their growth in neighboring areas of the adjoining inner cities. Demetrius was growing influential. Denard had also grown influential in his new role as diplomatic attaché to some of the most powerful and prestigious congressman DC had seen to that point in time. Dorothy had also reached a degree of success in the immediate DC area that her endeavors reached into neighboring states, duplicating networks. By the time Della and Isaac found out that they were expecting for the second time, having already brought a young Vaughn into the world four years prior. First Della had Vaughn, then two years later Dorothy gave birth to Taylor, then Della again gave birth to Langston two years after that.

The family was deservedly on the rise, and more than a few situations were coming together well across the board. Maybe there was a way to have predicted that events were about to transpire that would forever alter the trajectory of these lives connected to the Fortune Brothers forever.

Unknowingly, as Dorothy entered Della and Isaac's home, the assassin laid in wait, having followed her for some time intending to murder her viscously in cold blood, only to send her husband Denard the strongest message; His work has a way of following him home in ways he had never envisioned.

As a young Vaughn, Taylor and Langston played on the floor of the living room; The sisters had just finished their meal. They sat watching across the opening between both the living room and kitchen as Isaac washed dishes, straightening up whatever he felt was out of place.

With peaked interest, Isaac headed over to investigate the strange sounds coming from beyond the backdoor of their home. Beads of sweat glistened in the yellow light of the overhead bulb. His gaze focused on the task ahead. The cold brass of the doorknob itself surrounded by the moistening grip of his hand as he turned it open. The .45 ACP pistol firmly clenched in his other hand as Isaac peeked through the crevice created from being slightly pulled ajar. He saw nothing abnormal. This did not deter his curiosity, so he ventured further out into the backyard and the darkness that consumed it. Observing tactical awareness of his worst fears for the situation, and the tingling sense that more was unknown to him within the mystery of what had peaked his concerns as he progressed along the side of the house. After several moments of wandering the backyard area, Isaac returned to the rear door. Ironically, just as he re-entered the home, the door kicked in and four men dressed in all black full tactical military gear bursted through the door as the debris flung about. Almost just as instantly, a series of deafening sounds erupted from their awkwardly looking firearms. Riddling Isaac with the bulk of those shots fired.

Isaac went with peaked interest over to the backdoor to further investigate the sound like most men would have. Upon his arrival to the door, he slowly placed his left hand onto the knob gently using one finger at a time to lay grasp to the knob before completely holding it and transitioning that hold into a turning motion with his wrist as the door slightly and slowly opened while his right hand was firmly in the trigger guard of his .45 ACP Pistol. As the door grew from opening to slightly ajar, Isaac peeked from the right side of the door down the outside of the house in the left direction from the opened door. Then when he felt he was clear in that direction, he leaned out of the door and repeated the process down the other side of the house on the right side of the door. He then swung his gaze to the overall 180 degree opening in between areas of the back yard carefully, and slowly before taking a moment of cautious reflection regarding what he could see that would have justified having caused the group of noises that he had heard which brought him out to the rear of the house. After a few auspicious moments of contemplation, he turned back towards the rear door leading back into the house. Just then, at when he had turned to return to the home through the front door, four men, dressed in all black BDU clothing with assault rifles draped across their backs with their pistols waving through the room finding their target, pointed the barrels of their firearms along their path.

Then suddenly, "Pow, Pow,... Pow Pow" shots fired. The masked gunmen let off four focused shots into Della's abdomen and chest area, finishing with two more shots in her head as both Vaughn and Taylor witnessed from less than eight feet away. Langston at this point screamed and cry from the sight of seeing his mother fall lifeless to the ground with massive blood spewing out from the midsection of her limp body as her gaze ceased to have any resemblance of focus or awareness. Vaughn stood motionless in disbelief as he also watched his mother get shot, then fall lifeless to the ground. With his mouth slightly open in disbelief, all he could do was to place his arm out and grab Taylor from starting to get ready to sprint over to his mother as he saw the next gunmen set his focus on her. Then the rest of the gunmen opened fire on Dorothy with countless ammunition fired into her from several angles based on their positions taken in the room.

Then with futile efficacy Isaac had just darted into the house, screaming out his wife's name, hoping to hear her respond, so he would know where he needed to be next. As he rushed around the corner, his face was greeted with the bottom of the magazine extruded from the body of the pistol, as it was slammed up against his forehead immediately upon his rounding of the corner. Isaac staggered backwards and was then the new focus of the gunmen who had just finished shooting Dorothy. They released a barrage of rounds into him with no mercy for his incoherence after being struck quite hard moments earlier. Now with all the adults dead, blood everywhere, the team of assassins inspected the suppressors attached to their weapons, and then the rest of their weapons as one gunman still masked stood forward walking closer to the children now all nestled behind Vaugh who was staring right at the individual walking up to him as the masked man extended his arm to point his weapon onto Vaughn spoke and said,

"Your interesting"

As he drew closer to him with his aim.

"Fortunately for you, I need to leave and killing you suddenly disinterests me."

With Vaughn still standing in a position shielding both Taylor and Langston, he stood as the gunmen departed from the residence, each acknowledging him with blank stares as they left. Langston was furiously crying, and that was despite a weeping Taylor rocking him back and forth in his arms as he mustered any ability remaining within him to not crawl over to his mother's body and mourn over her as each of these young children had very well witnessed first-hand one of the most vicious home invasions turned massacres the city had ever seen. Taking along with it one of its more cherished leaders of the community.

Over forty-five minutes had elapsed, the three children had not left the room where both their Mothers had been just so brutally slain. In that time, they each spent it proportionately standing, and grieving over each of the bodies as they all struggled devoutly to comprehend how their whole understanding of home, or peace, had just been obliterated before their tender eyes.

So finally, after about forty-five minutes of just the young boys standing in disbelief, Mr. Hanover from next door had pulled into his yard returning home from his evening errands, but without the abnormal scene of his neighbors' door having been left wide open he would have never given it a second thought. It was evening time, and he was familiar with Isaac for quite some time now, and Della as well. Familiar enough to know that neither of them would have ever left that door wide open with the children in the house at this time of night.

So, like a good true neighbor, he investigated what could have been the explanation. As he entered the residence, it became instantly clear that something was not right. Broken pieces of the door scattered around the entryway and glass along with it were all the evidence he needed. He instantly regretted not bringing his firearm.

His mind raced now for finding anyone that had remained inside. As he cautiously turned the corner from the kitchen into the living room, he just stopped the room still reeked of gunpowder and stale air. Mortified by what he had seen, he reached into his pocket to retrieve his cellular phone so that he could summon the authorities. Midway into the call, there they stood unbeknownst to him, watching his entire set of movements the entire whole he'd been in the home. All three of them, standing there silently. Hurt and abandoned. Hanover concluded his call after signifying the address a second time, then took a deep laboriously long breath, and then walked to the children wondering what in God's name was he going to say to them after all of this madness? Having been close with the family provided them all some ease of conflict as they simply embraced around Hanover when he drew close and the four of them stood huddled up around him holding one another and waited for the emergency response unit to arrive. However, once that call was made it took little more than a few minutes before the sound of a vehicle outside screeching its tires as it must have tapped the curb just before it finally came to a stop.

It was Demetrius. He ran into the doorway accompanied by his driver, who also played a security role in his detail. Both toting firearms with Demetrius having an awkwardly intimidating pistol drawn and vigorously seemed through the front of the home. It was merely a moment before he came upon the three of them huddled around Mr. Hanover. Respectfully, once the children saw Demetrius, the tears poured, and starting with Taylor, who had been carrying Langston in his arms, now talk steps towards Demetrius who was already walking towards the group while he simultaneously holstering his pistol into the holster from which it came out near the small of his back, inside of his slacks. As this happened, more sounds of tires screeching and doors opening and being slammed shut from outside emerged. Then shortly thereafter, six other men dressed in black suits with black ties rushed into the house with their weapons drawn. Once the first of the men entered the living room and saw Demetrius, he grabbed onto the receiver from his lapel and notified someone on the other end that the Delegate was secure. Soon the Ambulance sirens grew sharper and more piercing as they drew closer. Coupled with the sounds of law enforcement that had arrived on the scene as well. Demetrius himself was momentarily not himself as he stood there physically consoling his nephews, while emotionally disturbed by having to look at Dorothy, Della, and Isaac laid out across the living room floor, and the blood they left behind.

They turned as a group under the direction led by Demetrius to leave the area, but Vaughn just stood there looking at his deceased parents still laying on the floor as teams of different members of the crime assessment teams started to flood into the home. As they started to move around and inspect the bodies and the overall crime scene Vaughn just stood and watched in grim disillusion. Demetrius called out to him a few times unsuccessfully until he left Taylor and Langston as he communicated to them using a mixture of nonverbal gestures, and facial expressions to stay back as he kindly and sorrowfully approached his nephew and gently placed his large right hand onto Vaughn's small left shoulder. With his hand in place, it was not until Demetrius began to increase his grip on the shoulder ever so slightly did Vaughn turn to him, now realizing he was even there. Demetrius was starting to break down and seeing his nephew so broken and devastated but stoic in his handling of these events here.

Demetrius tightened his grip on Vaughn's shoulder once again but slightly sharper while still gentle overall in sentiment as he spoke to his nephew,

"Nephew... We must leave them for now. Please come with me so that these people can take care of them now"

Although quite reluctant, Vaughn eventually decided it was indeed time to at the very least leave the home he knew up to this point in time. After these events, he knew if nothing else that it could never be home again. He and Taylor both agreed on this by travelling mentally to the same place at nearly the same time. As they were being escorted away with Demetrius into his personal vehicle, the two young boys both realized that it would never be a home to either of them again. Not after all of what they just experienced could it ever have been more to them than a source of immense pain and grief.

As they were all loading into the blacked-out SUV, a blacked-out SUV of a different model also pulled up and from within it emerged Khaleel. Those were his sisters- and brother-in-law inside as well. He ran up to the vehicle where he'd seen Demetrius load the boys into as he arrived. He somewhat frantically approached the rear car door where the four of them sat and engaged with Demetrius as he observed the distraught sadness that loomed in the vehicle.

"Where are my sisters?", "Where is Isaac?"

Khaleel asked with angst and disbelief in his voice. To which Demetrius somberly responded to his Brother-in-law uncharacteristically,

"Khaleel, they have been killed."

"WHAT!?" Khaleel screamed loudly in aggravated disbelief, seconds before he ran into the house. Demetrius waved to the response team supervisor at the door, signifying he was clear to enter as he yelled out to Khaleel,

"The coroner is collecting their bodies now. I am taking the boys back with me until we sort through all of this. I know you have to do what you have to do now, so come to the house"

All said with a distinct chance that most of none of it was heard since this was earth shattering information for anyone to just have thrown at them at the moment. Fortunately, that same supervisor had heard him completely, understood the circumstances and gestured back to Demetrius that he need not worry, and that he will make sure his message was relayed to Khaleel. As these events transpired, Demetrius closed the rear set of windows and gave his driver the permission to head towards his residence. The SUV pulled off from the curb it had been parked on top of and began its route to the location Demetrius had designated into the evening as utter chaos was just beginning back on Chester Street.

As the SUV container Delegate Fortune along with his three nephews had crossed the Anacostia River, the sight of the response units to the house recently departed could still be vividly seen. The reflection of the lights dancing across the river's water served as a backdrop to Demetrius in mid-call with his point of contact, attempting to reach his brother Denard to give him an update on the circumstances of the evening's tragic events. Already aware that Denard would have touch down in just three more days, he was reluctant to withhold these developments until then out of a combined sense of sheer respect with a pinch of painful embarrassment with having to deliver this news at all being the one expected to ensure the safety of the family in his absence.

As the SUV proceeded along its path surrounded by the ongoing bustling activities of the areas of the evening, the vehicle continued on its course with the lights flickering across the river as it rode along.

CHAPTER 4

"Preparatory"

Now with Langston and Vaughn, having gone to live with Khaleel in the massacre's aftermath of their beloved parents. It had been over four years as the family did their individual best efforts to readjust to life without both Dorothy or Della. Vaughn took exceptional grief in losing his Father whom he cherished most as his all-inclusive guide to eventual adulthood. Taylor also was quite affected by the loss of his Mother as well. Denard returned early, as expected because of the horrific news brought to him. He actually stayed home for two and half of those mentioned years until Demetrius convinced him that Taylor was cared for and better suited for him to continue what he had been doing for the country and periodically return to visit. He continued to speak on this until eventually Denard grew confident that it was best for all. Denard was involved in operations critical to the Nation and its overall mission abroad. Occasionally those interests included endeavors on domestic soil.

Denard sat with Taylor for many occasions over a period spanning over a month, getting as much time doing a variety of tasks and activities to prepare for the changes to his residency. Taylor appreciated the two years that he knew had all been for his benefit. He understood his Father's passion for the job he performed that had been explained frequently during some original, and more livid dinner meal events with Demetrius. The one unanimous sentiment regarding his father was closest to some type of comic book hero. He was valued by all who shared the table with them. This was unanimous even when they went out and about in the city. If they recognized him, the display of respect was immediate and displayed with little professional and sometimes military bearing for wherever they were when the greeting had occurred. Deep down inside, Taylor admired and idolized his Father like any son should at that age. Taylor secretly wanted to be just like him, however he was not found at all of attention his father received. That part he wanted nothing to do with. Eventually the day and time arrived where Denard was to fly out of the city, leaving Taylor behind to be raised in a larger part by his Uncle Demetrius. The three men travelled to the Airport together and sat together and shared a meal at the executive lounge. There wasn't much said during that meal, which was customarily odd for the three when dining together. Just the smell of their individual meal choices hovering faintly over and around the table, which had been overpowered by the sound of the silverware as it touched their respective plates. Somewhere in between, all of that had been some slightly audible echoes of Taylors Chewing. When he got a bit too loud Demetrius sent some facial expressions his way, then let it ride given the circumstances hovering over this meal like none before it.

Denard shortly thereafter, got himself a powerful hug from his son, like never. Taylor emphatically told him to be safe and that he loved him very much. Denard looked into his Brother's eyes then told him he was grateful. Demetrius told him he was doing what

he is supposed to do out of the strength of their bond. Denard stopped for just a second to look at Taylor once more, than disappeared into his gait towards his soon to be departing plane.

Demetrius and Taylor stood side by side as they watched him depart. Then solemnly they departed as well on their way to the vehicle, waiting for their return park by baggage claim. Demetrius could do this sort of thing. Taylor and his Uncle discussed the parameters of how this arrangement was to be conducted. There was much more flexibility than currently been accustomed to, but that it came with the cost of a higher accountability for his choices. Demetrius did his best to be as transparent with Taylor as possible to create a cohesive operating environment for them both to continue to grow and strive to improve upon themselves. He had much he wanted to impart upon him. Demetrius knew that in order for any of that to be remotely possible it would require for his Nephew to embrace him as Uncle who is the authority who can also wear the friend hat with the smoothest transitions when appropriate. This sort of thing brought him to the success he has. Being relatable and sincerely effective at delivering the harder message. Sometimes having the opportunity even to influence a change in mindset without manipulation, just another Fortune with the knack of understanding what a person is seeking. He often assisted many in getting there in faster fashion while picking up more than what they had initially expected to get along the way. The two of them soon discovered they had much in common regarding personality, while still having many other differences in preferences. Taylor admired his Uncle on a different plane than how he admired his Father. They got along well and much time had passed. Taylor fitted right into his new community while still keeping in touch with most of his original set of friends. Roughly about four years had passed,

Taylor was now ten years old. To a ten-year-old growing up in the South-Eastern quadrant of Washington DC, the park and city benches were just as alluring and exciting as they were statistically dangerous to venture out onto for prolonged periods of time. Watching all the men and women that were adored, and emulated throughout the entire neighborhood, and pretending that one day they too would have important conversations, and stories of street infamy amidst these benches for all the kids behind them in line to fantasize about in the same way, but even more. Still grasping for a path from his own personal tragedy while forcibly trying to get his mind wrapped around how success was going to be defined in his mind, let alone pursue it with the plan he felt most likely to yield him success for the effort. Only a teenager, and he'd already lost a tremendous sum from circumstances that he had no direct part in. Without having a Mother to call his own, and rely upon for that irreplaceable nurturing, he wondered what he would become, and whatever that wound up being, would that man be won his Mother would've been proud of?

Taylor would spend a substantial amount of time sitting on the bench close to his home, or an unoccupied bench just about anywhere in the city depending on where he was or had been doing. With so much on his mind, he sat for long periods of time just thinking about all that has happened, all that he had seen.

Sometimes as he would replay these scenes in repetition, attempting to better understand things more effectively. While often enough, on many other occasions he would find absolutely no satisfaction in doing so.

This was mainly because of the ongoing process of dealing with the shock, grief and trauma of having been separated from his mother so abruptly, and at such a young age, so angered by not understanding why he would never see his caring mother again in this lifetime. These were not only the kids who were cub scouts with him, they played little league sports with him. None of his other friends were poor, yet none of their families were wealthy either. The Fortune's although wealthy never lived visually above or even at their level of finance. A tradition of discretion passed through the lineage focused around the ideology that if one has attained wealth then they can build up those close to do the same and eventually the entire community, even more.

This was a serious family belief. A belief that eventually through action became a tradition- So what Taylor's Mother Dorothy would do is pull funds both from her activities, and with her employment endeavors along with funds from her husband to invest in buying and maintaining as much of the local commercial real estate as possible. Building to building as they would come available from owners divesting in the area and liquidating their assets in order to do so. Then she would put people in business through local knowledge of skills and services provided and the need for these services. Mrs. Fortune was the city's nurturing mother; it has needed all its existence.

Mrs. Dorothy essentially became her own chamber of commerce without the media attention or title. She just did it. Food drives, book drives, clothing banks were also staples to her foundations that were operated under the utmost discretion. Stitched into existence even deeper each time she would refer a neighbor or friend of a friend to a realtor she knew about an available property on the market, the referral to the loan director at any of the banks in the community that would be eager to do all they can to assist. These acquaintances came to find their current positions of opportunity through Mrs. Fortunes' network. Her passion to develop and to assist was seldom seen, and as a result the community strives and grew. Her discretion was so devout that she had all of her friends under her employ, and they never knew she was the person behind it all. All the checks were farmed out to be signed from one shell nonprofit to another. The passion foundations she was directly connected to also received its funding from groups associated with those shells not-for-profit organizations. With being a learned accountant, there was no need to have the massive amount of book-keeping by anyone else. That she would do primarily on her own- If she delegated out booking keeping work, it was done in the same fashion as everything else. So, in the very least, all the nosey and curious people around these situations could say she was an essential part of the company, and therefore it all made sense how she would know about the opportunities she would pass onto various people.

Before becoming Mrs. Dorothy Fortune, she was Dorothy Proffit. She was a member of the Proffit Family, a family that went back to the historical times of the revolutionary war. Both Families could be traced back to these times. Both families have been active in making this American existence furtive. The Fortune Family had been considered an institution within that community, so much more than just a family. The merger of the Proffit and Fortune Families had proven to have been essential and successful collaborations of two families as similar as they could be viewed as different. There were members of the Proffit Family that made the controversial choice to partake in the dealing of Narcotics during the nineteen forties. This seizure of an opportunity came as the reign of prohibition came apart, yet there were many within the family who not only shunned the decision to do so but also split the family apart because of those who chose the lifestyle that was outside the confines of the known laws. Ultimately, only a few members of the family-maintained ventures along this path altogether, Tension grew amongst the family. Overall, the family was an affluent and respected one. Educated and composed of independently wealthy people who got deep-rooted connections in the urban environment and within some Nation's more affluent communities as well. One family member in particular, his Uncle Khaleel Proffit. Uncle and brother to his deceased Mother, Dorothy. Khaleel shared a coincidentally similar background to that of his nephew. Khaleel introduced Taylor and his group of friends to life after Taylor's Mother Dorothy was murdered in cold blood in front of him while he was still a young boy.

Periodically as Taylor would sit amongst the people at one of the many benches, he found solace at, but accompanied with pondering of his insights on how the people walking by behaved. Wondering at first what they were thinking, why did they do the things he'd see them do, where were they traveling to and of course for what reason?

In time, Taylor grew to recognize these travelers for being from the community and those who were not. Eventually Taylor Fortune graduated from high school and worked for himself and dabble occasionally in other hustles. Something he picked up from spending a lot of time on those park benches was a keen skill in identifying needs and how to satisfy them. Taylor became a community concierge. Not locked into any set of items or services, yet rarely excluding services or the ability to get a wide and widening variety of products. The scarcer the desire was to get the higher the price. Whereas most of his friends made more specific choices and focused on what came with them.

Taylor was fortunate for countless reasons. The nephew of a career Senator, and the son of a Skillful Father who contracted his many skillets to the government for a significantly remarkable premium. Yet the family never migrated from the building where their residence in DC originated from. Yes, there have been significant renovations made to the once homely, now lofty estate like complex.

Tenants within only pay their own utilities based on their individual consumption. The building serves as an office and headquarters of Taylor's Uncle, Demetrius Fortune. The esteemed Delegate from the District of Columbia. Delegate Fortune was more hands on with Taylor than his father Denard; who performed many contract assignments a year that resulted in him living abroad most of the year. Demetrius was home every evening as his work rarely took him far from home for much long at all. Taylor had house staff that would see to his needs, but could not follow him successfully beyond the residence after he reached the age of twelve. He simply became too illusive for them to bother in doing so when he would evade their attempts swiftly each time once he set his mind to becoming skilled at doing so. Taylor was unique, so he did not allow himself to grow bitter with either his deceased mother, his absentee father, or his preoccupied life in Uncle. Instead, he sought as much understanding as possible about the elders he was responsible to report to with accountability for his choices. Even though neither one of his guardians would approve of every transaction he has involved himself into the more so trust his understanding of consequence as an aspiring adult.

At first Taylor did not know what either of his guardians did for a living and what it actually meant. All that was clear was they did a lot for more people than any normal person did, and he was astonished early on with the ability to remember each person or at least speak in specifics to their lives on a drop of a dime when they would resurface. With Demetrius close by, Taylor began early on, absorbing his behaviors. When they shared the dinner table with the seemingly endless stream of random to routine guests, Taylor would simply sit and listen to as much of their

conversations as he could follow before boredom would set in from not having a clue to what they were discussing. This changed drastically as he used that bewilderment to inspire him with his academics and to research as much that he could remember. He eventually began keeping a journal just for his determination to better understand what was spoken on in his presence, so although he did not speak or take part in these discussions unless invited into or asked a direct question, he was driven to at least not allow these exchanges to go beyond his awareness. When the conversation would routinely reach the segment where what was going on in the minds of the youth would approach Taylor would strategically use those moments to his benefit by asking a few questions himself that provided him with a better understanding of what entities would produce what goods and what industries stood to gain from a variety of different business scenarios. Ultimately expanding his understanding of the larger picture of what industries need from others, and how to more instinctively evaluate needs. Demetrius would be thoroughly pleased with his nephew's increasingly showed understanding of industry and commerce, so he would make it a point to ensure such a series of opportunistic seaways would take place.

Over the years these conversations became more strategic, and Taylor performed intellectual services for his uncle by playing more of a scripted role in these conversations. This role was obvious in tone, and became an additional delight to his guests to partake in the shaping of a young individual who could in fact be so young, yet versed in political communications and intellectual persuasion at such a young age. When the time had come for Taylor's graduation from high school, it was in mutual agreement that his next institution of higher learning would be Howard University. Close to home and an excellent educational opportunity.

Taylor took those dinner conversations along with the insight and information gained from them and turned his small enterprise into a formidable force with little to none direct competition because of his business servicing all imaginable needs for those who put a value on having their needs satisfied at cost. In his despair, he discovered what value was and how value had a different meaning to each of us in this unusual world. Rarely would he turn down an opportunity to capitalize on a lucrative opportunity. Early on, Taylor discovered that why a person sought after his niche services was more important information than what they claimed to have needed. So, he became a licensed private detective in his spare time after coming of legal age and worked alongside a mutual acquaintance of both his father and uncle as he fulfilled his apprenticeship before he could open his own independent shop. And with the additional privacy and confidentiality of doing such he brought up a few others he deemed trustworthy to extend his investigative reaches into anyone who would seek his concierge services. Fortuitous enough because he did so as soon as he could, he hadn't been manipulated in the course of his Enterprises activities.

It was that niche market enterprise that allowed him to pay for his Howard University education. His team of close associates that followed his advice and get their investigative licenses worked for him, and they made it their primary goal to get information regarding any member of the student body that was noteworthy to include a significant number of others who were essentially not. Identifying all that connects their targeted collective lists of people of interest was all that Taylor needed to get the most streamlined access to what he determined to be genuine power networking. He sought to become knowledgeable of what each association could produce and how to buy such a production from each encounter to further expand his ability to satisfy needs for a selectively wealthy clientele. He did however take many pages from what was known to him of his uncle's playboy by doing just about the same thing for people who could never monetarily afford his services, so with those services he requested a fresh set of currencies; influence. Gained through either bribery, and or extortion if need be. Occasionally a show of force was necessary when dealing with some less desirable the city had spawned into the community, and this sort of individual only understood and showed compliance to one thing which was the propensity of violence, and on rare occasions extreme violence. Growing up sitting on one park bench to another spending chunks of his days observing his community, he discovered that violence only caused more violence. So, Taylor decided that if he were to take his enterprise into any realm that involved violence, it had to be done with strategic excellence with the end game in mind from the thoughts that ultimately led to the first movie made. So, discovering inconspicuous methods to provide his services to people connected to the more powerful, and feared individuals in the community would benefit his strategy significantly. Not to mention that many of the more influential members of the area were well versed in the names of his Father and Uncle, the Fortune Family period. Since Taylor did not make his name his business, yet more so making his business his name when the two were connected, it became a successful acquisition of respect for not only Taylor, but his family as well. Taylor was already well known without being well known all across the DC area, so by the time he started college it was only the elite who was left on his list. Whereas he had already solidified his footing in the community amongst the average citizen during his adolescence. This method proved wise as it produced his desired results, and without pledging a fraternity, he was unofficially deemed the master of secrets on campus. Taylor would be there when a student, the child of a prestigious family, would be caught in a DUI Road check and know the group of officers manning the check well enough from their own moments of circumstance to evacuate them and their vehicle without infractions and documentation of their presence. The same would be done for any individual who would be evaluated as influential. Taylor grew an abundance of talent in redirecting a person's gained influence into being an influence that he could temporarily utilize for his purposes. In some cases, his utilization of their influence became more perpetual. Taylor had a way about himself where he could enter a room with great presence, engage with everyone and disappear into the same room when needed without exiting the room. He had a true understanding of how to share a spotlight, and even encouraged enthusiasm amongst those he chose to share with, again being able to coach and teach without coaching or teaching and dispersing without leaving. He always had four or five close associates along with him, and these people could darn near emulate this skill set. Although their respective roles in the engagement were not as prolific as Taylor's, but in order to move with him and be able to slide into the appropriate conversational window with the appropriate timing these individuals in his entourage had to be able to not only keep up, but stay in synchronization with Taylor as he pivots on a grain of rice. Failure to effectively do so would throw off Taylor's rhythm and illuminate him in ways he felt were undesirable and burdensome. This level of incompetence was thoroughly vetted out of his group through constant communication. Most of the members of his team had grown up alongside Taylor from the age of seven. Not all attended the school, but since the school was close to home and a bustling marketplace hosting a buffet for all varieties of opportunity it truly was beneficial to any business person to keep themselves connected to the pulse as it did just that pulsate day in day out. Taylor merely had a knack at identifying these societal arteries and which bore the closest connection to the heart of the city, community and in some cases establishment. Taylor kept a detailed series of journals in code and a series of journals that defined that code. Both kept in different bank safety deposit boxes on opposing areas of town. He would visit these financial institutions periodically to update their contents. These journals served as a log that insulated the body of work he had amassed over his growth. Demetrius Fortune was a role model in more ways than one. Once an active athlete, Demetrius did not participate in the intramural basketball activities like he once did. Taylor however learned how to play basketball from both his father and his uncle. Which in many ways were two different schools.

Denard was an above the rim player who spent a great deal of energy on his aggressive dribbling tactics to create opportunities in the lane to ultimately either produce a backdoor alley op or a dunk for himself, so he was an explosive player that had to be accounted for on any court he stood on. Whereas Demetrius was a below the rim player that mastered the art of ball movement and extensive range to mid-range shooting. A very deceptive threat all the same. When the two of these men played on the same court, it was incredible to watch. Their games would intertwine all but seamlessly. No confusion, not even much talking, just a significant amount of eye communication. If a person played with them, they had to keep their minds in the game, and in the game within the game.

A true sight to be seen, and as Taylor grew older, he could earn a spot-on court alongside both his uncle and his father before they stopped playing. Taylor learned how to play with the two of them together. It was important for him to show his ability to do so and to give them both as many opportunities to do what they both respectively loved to do while an on court in their favorite game situations. Taylor had that talent of understanding what people needed or wanted. He grew his enterprise with this understanding.

Growing up spending most of his time with his uncle Demetrius, he found himself obsessed with wondering what his father would do while he spent so much time away. Where Demetrius was consistent and somewhat mild mannered, Denard was gregariously outlandish and charismatic. People were drawn to his energy like nothing he'd ever seen, so he riddles himself in curiosity and anticipation for each time his father would return home. Vowing to his father that one day he would grow up and come along with him on one of his contracts. Denard encouraged this despite Demetrius's reluctance, but could not deter him, for Taylor was his son and not his own. Demetrius did however counsel his younger brother to at least encourage Taylor to graduate from college first.

What neither brother had known was that throughout the years Taylor had grown quite proud and attached to the small enterprise he had created there and became reluctant himself in letting it go. He had remembered that for as long as he could remember he'd been sharing with his father upon his many returns before his countless departures that he wanted to join him eventually, but as time had elapsed his passion to do so had not subsided more so became complicated. For the first time in his young life, he felt himself growing disharmonized about his direction. Knowing that in his heart of hearts he truly did still fantasize about potentially one day joining his father as some type of operative, fighting that real invisible fight with all the excitement, and the mesmerizing allure that came along with it. Taylor reluctantly had been increasingly hesitant to abandon his business endeavors at home. His enterprise had a movement of its own, and Taylor had grown increasingly fond of what he had started there.

So, the long night had broader his horizons into the new day, and after five years of arduous balance he maintained and even grew his endeavors to small beginnings in Baltimore, Philadelphia, and New York. Taylor also graduated from Howard with his JD MBA as he successfully tested a grueling dual major in business and political science with his law focus on international law.

As he celebrated his vigilance, and the accomplishments of his crew over their short tenure, finding himself even more reluctant to follow in his father's footsteps, yet conflicted about feeling so. It was still a powerful desire, but with the broadening opportunities before him with his current existing business affairs, he stewed uncharacteristically with a quagmire of a conundrum to be resolved. He had not felt this confliction over his direction since he was a youth. Despite his consternation, he knew where he stood the best chance of obtaining the clearest focus to better sort things out.

The next morning as he took one of his vehicles out of the parking garage under their building, and he visited the same park he once spent a significant amount of time at while he was attempting to make sense of obliteration of his young world as he had known it dealing with the tragic murder of his Mother, Aunt, and Uncle. The vacuum their departure created in his childish heart and mind was severe, and arguably still unresolved emotionally to date.

Eating breakfast sandwiches, he picked up along the way; he sat on that park bench, and as expected, found himself noticeably rejuvenated. Soothed in just being able to observe the city from that position; one passing car, baby stroller toting mother, occasional jogger, and bustling pedestrian at a time.

What Taylor did not know was his uncle Demetrius had long been aware of many of his extracurricular endeavors. It should definitely not have been a surprise for this to have been the eventuality of this trajectory because of the unrivaled influence and reach of the Delegate over a somewhat short tenure in office that anyone could have maneuvered on any level of consistency and sustainability without finding themselves well within his radar.

Through an unlikely mutual acquaintance, his awareness of

Taylor's activities intrigued him to investigate a little deeper into just exactly what his Nephew had going on. Demetrius was astounded by the manner in which his nephew had stitched together a vast network of influence from their building to reaching New York, Atlanta, Chicago, and even to include Miami.

This was more than impressive; it was monumentally captivating. Unaware of Taylor's internal struggle, whether to follow up on his longtime ambition to follow in his father's path, Demetrius started to more vividly visualize his nephew's potential in the larger scope of events developing domestically and eventually abroad. Realizing the eventuality of the natural dilemma this may pose for Taylor after he discovered just how vast of a network Taylor had created, while knowing that his nephew innermost desire or whatever amount of this desire had remained through the years to be a part of some vindictive effort to avenge the senseless murder of his Mother, Aunt and Uncle.

Demetrius had to find a process to bridge the gaps between what was discussed all these years and left out of the conversations regarding the actual activities involved within what his Brother really did. Taylor did not know the true nature of what his father did, nor why he was doing it, and for whom he did it for. Still fascinated with his nephew's accomplishments, and knowing that with his graduation still settling in, that Taylor must have been somewhere attempting to figure out his next move, or soon to be, if not convalescing from the lengthy celebrations from that previous weekend. Compelled to reach out to his nephew and see if he would share any of the details of his growing enterprise with him voluntarily. All while knowing with almost a certainty that his nephew had once desired to be a part of similar work to that of his Father when he was much younger, and less seasoned. Demetrius wondered if maybe this had been the moment to reevaluate the idea of providing some incentive to see for himself how coming into the fold at this point would be good for him in the big picture, and immediately beneficial. He strongly hoped that his nephew would feel comfortable enough to speak frankly and confide in him. He and his father needed him a great deal and apparently, he had produced an impressive resume for the opportunity on his own whether he had been aware. With no doubt to either his father or uncle, his potential was unlike others, and possibly truly something special was in their midst.

With Taylor graduating from Howard and not spending as much time at the residence as he once had, it was becoming less predictable when the two men would cross paths to speak as it once had been. So, he pulled out his cell phone, then paused, and sat in mid-thought before he started the call.

Taylor, seeing the caller id, answered his phone with jubilation and a celebratory tone, shouting "Happy Birthday UNC!"

"I was definitely going to call you this morning!"

After a few more rounds of pleasantries, that moment in a telephone conversation where the purpose of the call had yet to be specifically announced, but still expected to be made clear. This development arrived with an awkward silence. Demetrius remained coy to his general purpose in contacting him as he did his best to extend the pleasantries and small talk for as long as he could do so. Oddly enough Taylor was not fond of beating around the bush being the fast-paced mover he had grown into, and his Uncle had known this already, so this approach made Taylor slightly worrisome and uneasy with the direction the conversation was following.

What Demetrius had not been aware of was how Taylor had been aware of their mutual associate's attempts to disclose the nature of their past endeavors, but it was Taylor who sent that person to do so. Taylor knew that from that individual's divulsion, eventually his Uncle would more than likely find himself interested and motivated to seek further knowledge into these endeavors of his.

Both men had internally acknowledged the unspoken tension growing in the call simultaneously. After a medium amount of time suffering through more small talk, both talking about everything except what was on both of their minds to discuss. Eventually Taylor simply said to his Uncle that if he needed anything from him, he was always available to him."

To which his uncle acknowledged the sentiment in a grateful gesture of smirking and nodding his head before he replied to his nephew.

"I will get out of this office soon yet and come find you for perhaps lunch one afternoon. Matter of fact, why not today, Taylor? We need to catch up."

Demetrius then waited for a response. There was a gasp of long silence, then a brisk response from Taylor. "Sure, what time did you have in mind?"

"Will one thirty work for you?"

"I can make that work, Unc,"

"Great, can you come by the office and we can find a place together?"

"Sure, Uncle D, consider it done. Looking forward to seeing you"

With both Demetrius and Taylor engaged in their separate endeavors, and having confirmed the appointment to meet later in the day, Demetrius found some relief in at least setting the stage to evaluate his nephew in his reaction to what he wanted to share with him.

While Taylor was slightly uneasy with the call and the many questions it created in his active mind as to the awkwardness of the conversation. Both went about the activities of the day, still able to have been addressed in the allotted time before the lunch appointment. Although mildly distracted, Taylor took to the streets, handling some matters with as much efficiency as possible before one in the afternoon. This schedule would afford him enough time to get to his Uncle's Office. Then Taylor had to think, and he remembered he wasn't certain which office he was expected to meet him at, knowing that his Uncle used two primarily. So, he texted his uncle quickly to make sure of the office location for their initial meetup. Before a minute or two passed, he received his response confirming the location as "not on the Hill".

The time was already about one fifteen. The park was abnormally quiet across the street from his Uncle's satellite office, and there were few young children, alone or accompanied by either their caregiver or parent playing nearby, as there would normally have been. After taking notice of this random visual discrepancy, he strolled into the building where he had met his uncle coming out from inside the elevator, which had just opened its doors out into the lobby.

The two men cheerfully greeted one another like there was no conversation pending. Approaching the foyer of the lobby, waiting for clearance from Demetrius's security team pending verification of acceptable status pertaining to the immediate area beyond the entrance of the building, done simultaneously with their arrival at the doorway.

The smooth transition of late model matte black on black Cadillac

Sky Captain sports utility vehicle suddenly springing up to the curb just outside the entrance; promptly followed by two other Late model Escalades from off Eleventh Street and parked along the First street side of the park with the Sky Captain's position in front of the other two.

The last vehicle came to a stop when a third escalade sped to the front of the motorcade party, cornered with the front end of the Sky Captain without pulling in.

In typical fashion, the executive protection specialists of Delegate Fortune moved through formations as they descended from their armored vehicles with a sleek and minimized spectacle of disciplined precision in preparation to receive the Delegate into his vehicle.

Taking all of about six to seven full seconds, once prompted,

Taylor and Demetrius then entered the rear cockpit of the Sky Captain- as the doors were closed behind them. The vehicles then took off from the curb as the gentlemen in the rear cockpit decided where this meal and this conversation was going to take place.

"McCormick's on Crystal," suggested Taylor.

"Sounds about right with me. We have some celebrations to acknowledge." Demetrius had replied.

Just before the motorcade could pull off from the curb, a woman of medium build and middle age had approached the lead vehicle requesting to say a word to the Delegate. This information was relayed to Demetrius via radio and Demetrius, being who he was to the community, rolled down his window, then signaled to the woman for her to approach the vehicle. Before she could get any closer, a security team member had stepped in between herself and the vehicle's window as to say in her silence that she had drawn close enough to the Delegate unannounced on the street.

She gasped to speak with a visible distress over her demeanor as she spoke briefly and softly as if it was painful to even speak.

"Delegate Fortune...it is me, Mrs. Rhodeson from East Washington

Heights? Over off Branch Ave. When can I come see you, Delegate Fortune? I have something that I really hope that you could assist me with. I am not clear minded right now because of my situation, but at the moment I can only hope I am being premature in seeking you out. My instinct tells me otherwise, so prayerfully I am wrong, and only wasted a moment of your time. But if I am not, then I will definitely need your involvement."

To this Demetrius, now intrigued, responded, "Sounds serious enough for me. I will return to the office around three this afternoon. Come see me and we will talk then."

Again, the motorcade pulled further away from the curb. This time with success as Demetrius finished rolling the window on his nephew's side all the way back up. As the vehicles pulled off along their way to their destination, both Taylor and Demetrius spent those initial moments handling some last-minute communications via their mobile devices before putting them down and to the side in the ceramic cup in the center console designated for them.

Again, they spoke and exchange some small talk. Taylor started this with,

"Wow, Uncle D, you stay connected and approachable out here.

That was great to see. You just keep adding on to your network.

Always remarkable to see."

Demetrius quickly responded, "Yes, that was odd indeed. I am looking forward to getting to better understand exactly what is going on there, and what has Mrs. Ortiz so rattled. This office has broadened my shoulders more than I ever would have envisioned it being capable of. I am blessed because of this. Your ability to see things like you just showed enhances that blessing more than you may be able at this moment to realize. Your parents are very proud of who you have grown into, one I am certain of while the other I know is."

The two men sat in silence for a few moments as the vehicle proceeded along its path briskly through the bustling city from one community through to the next. Just shy of approaching the Frederick Douglass Memorial Bridge, Demetrius spoke once more by simply staring.

"Congratulations on your phenomenal accomplishment, I am also not only very proud of you, but even more proud of the young man you have grown to be at this stage of your life. You are breathtakingly a significant source of happiness for me."

Again, Taylor brought to an emotional climax as he shielded his face skillfully from his Uncle, looking out the vehicle on his side at the Anacostia River, looking down towards the Virginian coastal border. While he had turned his cheek before the one or two tears he had shed covertly descended from his left eye onto his shoulder. Tears he wiped away with misdirection, while putting on a pair of sunglasses he pulled from their sleek case from within his pants pocket. At the opportune moment, as the sun snuck into the vehicle sharply and swiftly long enough to coincidently mask his need for a distraction. Taylor took a moment to better appreciate that distraction silently, as he continued to bask in its cover while he recovered his countenance. As the vehicle cascaded through first the Navy Yard, then Capitol Hill and the Waterfront before crossing over the Potomac River into

Pentagon City, where they finally arrived at their destination in Crystal City at

McCormick's. Again, the EP team went through the subtle process of getting the delegate and his guest out of their vehicle and into the establishment while being the least noticeable in doing so.

With the Delegate being a usual patron to the establishment, the both of them were discreetly sat at one table he liked as they entered the dining room area. As they pulled out their own chairs and found relaxation in the comfort of their seats, the wait staff had just made their approach in the expected request for their drink orders.

Demetrius responded,

"I will have a crown with an Arnold palmer on the side."

Taylor also spoke shortly after being asked what he had wanted,

"Actually, I think I am going to try some crown as well, and may I have a glass of cranberry juice on the side?"

Demetrius gestured to the lead of his EP team to come over to him. Briefly they discussed some matter, and as the team lead departed from Demetrius's side, he made a few subsequent communications nonchalantly amongst the members of the team in the dining area with them before utilizing his communication device on his lapel to communicate something to the members of the team not inside the dining area. Demetrius then spoke to Taylor.

"Nephew, I hope you have room for some wonderful food today?"

Just as this was said, the senior chef and his assistant came from the back of the house out into the dining room to the astonishment of the other patrons also having their lunch. They walked in moderate yet visible excitement over to the table where Demetrius and Taylor were located. The Tandem greeted the Delegate and express their gratitude in his choice for his lunch being at their establishment. The Demetrius and Taylor were discreetly offered a wider choice of menu items that coincidentally included many items that not only Demetrius had been strongly fond of, but items that Demetrius had known over the years of their cohabitation that Taylor had been quite fond of as well.

The both of them glossed over the menu in appreciation for the specialized effort to satisfy them. More so Taylor than Demetrius, who had obviously arranged for this situation to take place as it was occurring. Finally, both gentlemen make their decisions known to the eager Chefs. As the both of them sat in silence briefly as the Chef's both finished sharing their pleasantries with their Delegate, the moment of silence extended, until interrupted by Taylor who just said,

"So, Uncle D, what do we really need to discuss? What is it that is so pressing on your mind for us to speak on? I'm actually quite curious."

To this Demetrius sat silent with an awkward grimace across his face, almost at a loss for words.

"I am glad you asked. One thing for sure that I just need to say with no way of understating the sentiment of it all is that I am immensely proud of you as a man. After that, I need to congratulate you on quite an impressive run at Howard. Now Perhaps with that said we can now take a moment," his pause brief as he continued, "If I may speak to you about the future. Possibly what your future can be. I am sure that you know I am and have been well aware of your activities in the city and some of those beyond this city as well through the years Taylor."

At this Taylor expressed a facial response that showed he was not surprised, but intrigued to where this portion of the conversation was about to venture into. This development was an interesting one for Taylor because until now their relationship was one of minor to elder. This topic however transcended that relationship into the merging of the adult version of how Taylor grew into communication. less reverence and more pragmatism are the best summarization for the differences in tone and demeanor. Although respectful to his Uncle always without interruption, Taylor took a moment upon hearing what his Uncle had said last, to reposition himself in his chair to a more mature and more discerningly diligent position, altering his mannerisms to match that change in posturing.

Demetrius, impressed while he spoke, noticing this shift in demeanor and positioning of his nephew within his seat without breaking his line of thought, as he continued to speak to him responding to his question as thorough and concise as his experience would have him do.

"Yes. I know about your entrepreneurial endeavors since middle school. I have found much delight and perhaps some moderate shock in other moments as I became privy to the overall scope of your venture. I think that what you and your friends have created is nothing short from utterly remarkable."

Taylor interrupted as Demetrius took a dramatic pause at his last utterance with slight condescension, "But... What do you think can be improved Uncle D? I feel like there is definitely a but coming in this"

Demetrius continued to acknowledge the enormity of his creation, "I mean the time to not only conceive such an undertaking, but to also successfully implement it methodically, and swiftly over a moderately brief span of time required a unique skill-set to be brief. Your expressed understanding of things could be potentially further expressed in other endeavors."

Taylor took a moment after his Uncle had completed his sentenced and paused himself to look into his Uncle's eyes as if to gather his thoughts for that quintessential Taylor Fortune response that was new for his Uncle to most likely see, whether he had heard about this sort of thing in whatever report he was getting on his maneuvers or not.

Then Taylor gave his response, "Further expressed? Are you speaking on what it sounds like you are speaking on Uncle Demetrius?" to which Demetrius responded quickly.

"Why yes I am Taylor That is exactly where this conversation is heading. No need to respond today. I will definitely need you to think on this for quite a while whether it will be a yes or no, a maybe or a never."

Demetrius then continued to speak to his nephew,

"For you to construct such an enterprise tells me that in the time it took for you to do so that it required determination and grit, vision and perseverance. The degree of interpersonal complexity of managing such a multifaceted venture that depends upon the managing partners to effectively and shrewdly maneuver through the much darker side of the population. Their desires, shortcomings, and their varied agendas, not to exclude some more unspeakable evils still necessary to navigate through to manage such an endeavor such as yours. So yes, as far, you are already doing much of what will be required of you to find success in that field."

Now Taylor sat silent as he listened to his Uncle with intensified curiosity. Demetrius took the cue and continued to speak,

"What me and your Father would prefer that you understood is that there is absolutely no success like that in which you have found and capitalized on here or gained in this world without adversely creating some less and other more formidable adversaries. Because of the complexity and far-reaching elements of what you've created, you have already sparked quite a few dangerous adversaries worthy of your recognition and respect. If just in the acknowledgement of their prowess and potential vulnerabilities they could impose upon you traveling unbeknownst to their existence and their respective reach. An affiliation with the entity we refer as the Under Shadow, whom mostly we are aware of, has been leveraging protection, and insulating you and your associates from these very real increasing threats to what you have perceived all these years as peaceful conditions. These parties have allies as well that move in opposition to your allies, and our aligned interests. Interests and motivations change like does the sunrise and sunsets of days past. We all fall under the same revolving door that turns into perpetuity while the people feverishly scramble over the increasing scarcity of power, property, and wealth available. This tightly balanced rotation of these resources is quite intricate, yet ever developing, and severely menacing as it continues to develop."

Taylor, uncharacteristically aghast, but undeterred, spoke up during the pause between his Uncle's words, returning reverence.

"Why would I abandon what I have fought so hard to build here,

Uncle D?"

"That's just its Nephew, I am not, nor is your father asking for you to cease in your activities here. We both believe that you can do more with what you have created. Take it to the next level and a few beyond there."

By this time their meals arrived, and the two men now slightly famished with appetite from their brief discussion dug into their entrees.

The both of them dug into their meals and discussed the matter no more. They spent the rest of the time examining the details of Taylors Graduation and journey through the hallowed halls of Howard, the alma mater of His Uncle. Demetrius enjoyed the company of his nephew immeasurably.

CHAPTER 5

"Harvest"

Taylor was just getting back to one of his satellite offices that he had across town. This one was in the rear of a coffee shop near Fourteenth street and Pennsylvania avenue.

It was owned and operated by a small Nicaraguan couple, Hector and Maria Cosnuela. Taylor helped them both find better progress in their citizenship pursuits by obtaining for them a more effective lawyer. Taylor met Hector while he was still in high school.

Hector was a store clerk in one of the smaller corner grocery stores in the neighborhood close to where he had been attending school. Taylor would converse with Hector at great lengths regarding a variety of day-to-day topics, from politics to neighborhood concerns. It was during these times that Hector shared with Taylor how he had fled Nicaragua when there was much civil unrest while reluctantly being forced to leave his new wife behind, so that he would come to America and establish something for them both to have a fresh start here and then raise a family. Taylor was inspired by these stories for Hector, and the two became closer. Eventually developing a friendship. What came after middle school for Taylor was his early entrepreneurial development and maturation into seeing some of what he felt necessary to get his grander plan off the ground. Hector was his bi-lingual partner in many of those initiatives, always getting a piece of the cut from deals his services made the difference in.

As time went by Hector saved his earnings and brought his wife to the states and they had their first child. Taylor became aware early in their association that Hector had prior experience farming coffee beans back in Nicaragua. So, Taylor propositioned Hector and his wife Matia into running a coffee shop in town that he would finance and establish for them with an adequate share of the profit. During construction, Taylor had several state-of-the-art additions made to the plans. These additions included an office and small conference room for him in the rear with an entrance of its own. This location was the first to be constructed with their operational needs in mind. Taylor would often conduct much business here and an occasional meeting with some more affluent members of the political community.

Spunk and Ox, more professionally known to their associates as respectively Thomas Lillard and Vincent Rizzo were at the coffee shop preparing for a few meetings that they had scheduled there later that morning. Thomas handled many of the accounts and the clients attached to their respective areas of interests to their enterprise. Whereas Vincent took responsibilities over other areas. This was also a similar case regarding the responsibilities of

Eugene Gutierrez, known amongst the crew as Geno, and Paul Tifton, who went by Poot to the crew. Last but not least, their unofficial intern had always been Langston Proffit, the younger brother to Vaughn Proffit. The Cousins of Taylor Fortune, who were essentially more like his brothers.

This has especially been the case since the vicious murders of both Langston and Vaughn's parents to include Taylor's Mother. Langston stuck to Taylor since their youth, and despite having a more robust personality in areas differing from Taylor, their differences had never prevented them from growing even closer through the hard years after the massacre.

The crew had more than a dozen office spaces across the city, established in very similar roots to the coffee shop of the fourteenth. Each satellite had much activity within it. These locations not only stood as occasional meetup points but also logistic centers overseeing the management of the countless businesses that were maintained by the operation.

Taylor arrives back at the coffee shop on the Hill and finds Geno and Spunk taking a meeting. He didn't interrupt them; however, they could be seen through the one-way glass.

Their clients did not have access to some technological tools that they had available to them, so while their clients could not see beyond the glass between them and outside of the conference room, Geno and Spunk had special contacts made to enable them to do just that and a few other things within the collection of office spaces in the network. As they had seen Taylor was in the office, they attempted to take a moment to speak with him until he saw this and gestured with his hand slightly and discreetly for them to continue what they had been doing. He then proceeded to the back office and sat behind the desk, and reached for the VoIP handset as he simultaneously collected his thoughts about who he needed to call first, why, and how to accomplish his purpose in the call.

"Good Afternoon, thank you for calling GeoCodex industries. My name is Agatha. How may I direct your call today?"

Voiced the receptionist.

"Yes, and thank you, Agatha. Calling to speak to Eric Tipowski. I believe he is expecting my call."

Was Taylor's Response to Agatha.

"Yes, Mr. Fortune, indeed you are correct, and I will transfer your call over now if you do not mind the brief hold."

Taylor then replied, "Not a problem. You have a brilliant afternoon, Agatha."

Taylor then waited as the melodic tune of the music playing in the background played gently from the handset's speaker. At this moment Taylor pressed the button that allowed for the call to be placed on speaker once he returned the handset to the docking port. Shortly after doing so, Eric took the line and began his entrance to call by exclaiming, "Mr. Fortune! What a most pleasant surprise indeed! Have you been able to source that item for me- at the desired quantities? Assuming that you have since we are speaking this afternoon."

With the opening left in the silence after Eric had spoken, Taylor responded,

"Yes, to both. Yes, to the discovery, besides the desired quantities. With more quantities also available in the future if the need for such should arise. However, because of the added effort in which it is needed to secure these items for you, hopefully we find common ground on what the new offer will be. Primarily, to provide you with value in this arrangement it is with high hopes both parties walk away satisfied. The reason you sought me out versus the lack of willingness to negotiate offers by any competitor."

A slight pause impregnated the air after Taylors' voice grew slightly firmer, and a tad bit colder where Eric's difficult breathing could be faintly distinguishable. The Eric coughed on an attempt to speak, cleared his throat before slowly annunciating his words,

"I am certain we can come to some agreeable figure."

Taylor responded so quickly to Eric's comment the timing would have any eavesdropper assuming he had interrupted his final syllable as it had been uttered as soft as it had been almost in concession.

"I will have Geno pay you a visit through the usual process."

Then he told Eric to have a fine evening before ending the call. After this Taylor looked through his phone for a moment, then attempted to start a next call when Geno knocked on the door, gesturing for permission to come inside. Taylor gave him the nod to come inside and then greeted him with a grin and immediately gave him an update on the situation regarding Eric Tipowski.

"Eric is ready for collection and delivery, so we will need you to follow up, and make that happen through the established channels. Preferably tonight."

Geno responded with haste and enthusiasm,

"Without question, Spank. Spunk just wrapped up that client from across the street that works on the Hill, for that congressional representative I was telling you about from the other day."

Taylor's eye briefly lit up, and he became excited in his demeanor as he exclaimed,

"That's what I need to see! That's the work we need around here! That was solid work Ge-no, Y'all killed that."

As Taylor spun around halfway in the high-quality black leather office chair before he got up from inside of it and gave Geno a high five.

Just as Taylor finished congratulating Geno, Spunk was coming to the door. As he smirked saying,

"He came in here and told you, right? I knew it. Yeah, we did that.

I think there is on that tree too. Also, I had run into Vaughn on

the way here, and he had made mention to the two of y'all linking up this evening at the lounge. Told me to make sure Poot, Geno and Ox were going to be there too. Also told me, "hold already spoken to Langston."

"Sounds Good"

Responded Taylor, as he checked his mobile device as if to look for missed calls or messages. Taylor, once through looking over his device, looked square in each of their eyes and spoke with motivation,

"Well, I will see the two of you later this evening. We all have things to attend to before then anyway, and we definitely won't get any of that done standing here. Also, we will get more into this evening, but I am strongly leaning towards taking on some additional work from my Uncle in the coming months. I may have to take off here and there. These trips may take me away from DC too. This opportunity will enhance our operations and stretch out our reach."

With that remark, Taylor took a second or two to establish eye contact with each of his people to nod in confirmation. Then both Spunk and Geno knew that the celebration was over for the moment, and it was back to the grind. The three of them left the skeleton crew of staff assigned to this location in the office and went their separate ways out the private exit to finish up what they each still had left to get done for the day.

Taylor was a recent graduate from a locally prestigious university, and seen by most of the individuals with power, influence and resources from the city as a Dependent of one of the most influential public servants in the region. Despite his desire for spectacle, this was a big deal. A Taylor reluctantly understood that any public figure, or former guest who had previously sat at that table in his Uncle's home, and bore witness to any section of his development into young adulthood had better make some spectacle or gesture of congratulation to him if they wanted to remain in the good graces of his Uncle who wielded a mighty legendary political long-sword.

Not to have it confused, Taylor did not feel that his reluctance to encourage or partake in public demonstrations of celebration or congratulation themed conversations as being ungrateful. Rather, his views on public displays of the like could start with the right motivations and quickly turn in genuine. Something he strongly disapproved of. So similar to one of his meeker former high school freshman classmates sleeking through the hallways with prowess of a professional cat burglar, Taylor walked to his vehicle for the day in strong expectation of going unnoticed and unapproached. As he slipped into his sedan, he felt a moment of accomplishment as he discreetly closed his car door. That elation however was short-lived, as he sat in the driver's seat, realizing that he had yet to pay an important visit to one of his higher valued clients, while additionally a colleague of his Uncle on the Hill.

Knowing that would definitely leave him walking directly into the path of spectacle, he considered catching the assemblyman at his home. Then he also realized that if he had, the next dilemma would have surely been being quilted into staying for dinner at the current hour, and he didn't have time for any of that. After some calculation, he finally pulled off from the curb accepting that he could pick back up on that mission to reach out too early in the morning and get a visit to the Hill out of the way, and all the public displays of his achievement.

With the usual high flow of vivid imagery related to what he needed to accomplish, and the multitude of variations that these positions could develop swirled through his mind. As he maneuvered through the neighborhoods between the coffee shop and his loft near Lanier Heights, he continued to visually sift through his options in his mind. Once home, he set the vehicle's security protocol to high as he handed off his keys to the valet attendant for the property.

"Franklin, please put her in my spot, numbered four"

The attendant nodded, then went about his way after wishing

Taylor a good evening. Taylor responded in kind with gratitude.

Taylor was quickening his stride as he drew closer to the elevator that opens out into his residence. The elevator attendant and Taylor shared a great deal of history. It was Taylor who played a large role in securing that employment for Jonathan, whom he'd known for most of his early youth. Their Mothers were quite close. However, while at the residence in plain sight of other guests and residents, they kept a non-familiar appearance up. Occasionally

Jonathan would come into the unit when summoned, and the two would break the routine and speak more transparent to the true nature of their association. The both of them had a strong respect for the discrepancy required for them both to minimize if not eliminate any unnecessary scrutiny or vulnerabilities that could arise from celebrating the degree of their companionship publicly. they both served one another far better, keeping that detail quiet in the building.

Taylor showered, selected his attire for the evening's scheduled events, then he picked up his mobile device off the podium and called the front desk.

"Yes, Good evening to you Samuel. I am leaving shortly and will need my vehicle from slot numbered two."

Samuel greeted Taylor,

"Yes Mr. Fortune. Thank you for using the Valet Caddy and have a wonderful evening."

Taylor then spoke to the digital assistant service associated with his mobile carrier.

"I want to reach the kitchen at the Lounge..."

The digital assistant responded,

"Confirm, The Lounge Restaurant in Washington DC on I street?"

"Yes. That is the establishment"

Taylor responded.

Once connected to the establishment via telephone, Taylor spoke with familiarity with the woman whose voice he immediately recognized once she spoke into the phone.

"Vivian? Is this you I am speaking with?"

To which the woman gleefully responded,

"Yeah baby, this is me honey, I see Vaughn and Langston are here tonight. Will you be here as well?"

Taylor was pleased as he continued,

"I am on my way, and I'm starving at that!"

"What do you want to eat, baby?"

"Let me have some sautéed spinach, some steamed broccoli, and a large T-Bone, medium rare! Thank you, Ms. Vivian,"

"No problem, Spanky baby. I'll have that ready for you in about twenty minutes. Will that work for you? How long are you from getting here?"

"That is a good time. I should be there by ten. That will give me a few minutes to speak and greet the guys first. I'll come through the kitchen on the way in so you know I'm there." responded Taylor as he was turning through a corner, closing in on the location.

Taylor swiftly drove around a couple of additional intersections before arriving at the lounge. He cautiously pulled around to the rear of the establishment. As Taylor made his way through the back of the house, he greeted Vivian with a kiss on the cheek as he reached into a pan and grabbed a taste of something that caught his eye as Vivian swung playfully at him to stop messing around in her kitchen. Once he hit the main floor, he sleekly maneuvered to the private room reserved for the group he had expected to meet.

With music blaring in the background, there was a slight moment of vacuum, as he opened the door into their reserved room where music had not been coming from with the loud echo of the music behind him. As Taylor entered the room, he realized that most of them had been standing and he was then greeted by the crew affectionately and in robust loudness. a Loudness that rivaled the intense volume just beyond in the lounge area. After Spank and

Poot ran up on him and dapped him up, Vaughn then approached Taylor walking slowly, finally coming toe to toe with his cousin extending his arm after a quick moment of silence and a blank expression on his face. An expression that suddenly broke into laughter. Then they embraced one another. Geno walked up to them both and gave Taylor a flash drive. Stating,

"This came from Rudolph and Megan, over on Silver Hill."

"Oh, that was fast."

Was Taylor's brief response as he and Vaughn made their way to the table to sit on the bar stools. In tune with Taylor's calculation, the door was slung open quickly as Vivian came into the room carrying Taylor's plate. She was followed by a hostess carrying drinks for Taylor as well. All the men in the room had joyfully displeased facial expressions upon their faces as these events transpired.

With a deliberate disregard for their facial activities, Taylor searched for a pepper shaker. Once he located it, pulling it closer to his position, he situated his napkin just so on the side of his warm plate. Vivian gave him a kiss on the cheek, then rubbed his head affectionately with her hand as she looked around at the rest of the men in the room, acknowledging their shock before she departed the room with a distinct smirk on her face.

As the door closed, the men roasted and interrogate Taylor about how he gained a plate with how he just arrived, as they've all been there.

With a mouth full of food, and a sneer on his face that seemed to find difficulty in speaking while also trying to enjoy his meal, that because of the looks of his expression was remarkably more enjoyable with each additional bite. With eating additional bite, and the elation over his countenance as he continued to eat amongst them created more of a roasting from the group. Spank and Langston almost simultaneously chimed in, almost yelling out;

"Now how did she know to bring you all that? You just got here! That's the shit we are talking about!"

Taylor, still thoroughly enjoying what was becoming less and less of his meal, took a moment to reach into his pocket, pull out his phone, put the device on the tabletop, then make an inaudible remark with his mouth full of food. Once this was done, he pointed to the phone, gesturing that it was the answer to their incessant questioning. After his gesture and mumbled remark, Taylor resumed his devouring of the food brought to him.

As he was coming to the last few bites, Vaughn, who had been sitting next to him had realized his cousin had obviously been quite hungry as he reached over and grabbed his shoulder gently then speaking to him simply said in a very soft but stern voice,

"Are you well now? I'm definitely going to need your attention, T."

Some guys left the room to catch up with Vivian to get something to eat. Taylor remained in the room with Langston, Vaughn, and Geno. Geno had made his way over to the table where Taylor had just finished his meal. Geno leaned onto the tabletop to listen more closely as Vaughn spoke.

"Well, you've gone and done it now, haven't ya?"

Taylor, slightly stifled in peaked anticipation how his thought was going to complete itself as Vaughn continued on.

"You went and finished that degree! You realize that without that schedule to keep you occupied that you just may find yourself bored really quick?"

To that, Taylor dropped his head in brief laughter before loudly responding to Vaughn.

"Man... I'm actually sitting here with some real shit to to tell you and you're playing."

Vaughn's facial expression did slightly change from his smirk frown to a look of increasing curiosity. Geno, however, was still finding the anti-climactic moment humorous. Mainly because he was aware of the subject that Taylor was referring to. He also knew their relationship and expected most of the occurrence.

Before Vaughn responded, he glanced over at Geno and realized that Geno must have already known whatever was about to be discussed as his facial expression did not seem as eager to find out what Taylor was getting at. Now Vaughn grew even more curious and less patient to find out what everyone else at the moment seemed to already know. After a brief pause where both Geno and Taylors blank expressions intensified his lack of patience to where he blurted out with a chuckle of humility,

"Ok, you win asshole. The anti-climactic award goes to you now.

Put me on already. What's the deal?"

Now Taylor smirked with smug reassurance as Geno laughed some more. Taylor took his hand and reached out for Vaughn's shoulder and patted him there with his hand, consoling him as he continued to smirk in response to his concession.

"Ok, Twirl! get on with it, Spank! You won already."

Taylor, now no longer smug or smirking, got up from his seated position and moved his plate, utensils, and napkin to the smaller end table closer to the door. As he approached the door walking backwards facing them both he spoke,

"As usual, Vaughn, you're right on the pulse of things. I'm done with school. The business is growing, and I may have found the boat to take it and all of us along with it over the great ocean between what we have now and that next level. I know that you and I historically move to different sectors of activity. I won't even beat around the bush. I will definitely need you watching over things with my guys from time to time as I iron some things out."

Both Langston and Vaughn approached Taylor, Langston standing behind his older brother as they reached him. Vaughn squinted his eyes and wrapped his hands around each other as he prepared himself to speak;

"So, your next move is to make moves with Uncle Denard and Demetrius? that's your next move, right? It's the only thing you would do that would take you away from your business and leave any part of it to me to watch over Taylor..."

Taylor's stance became more confident, communicating to both

Langston and Vaughn that Vaughn's interpretation was definitely on the right trail. Now Vaughn, turning to Geno with slight annoyance, spoke out to him,

"Are you aware of what that next level will bring with it? Are you ready for that?"

Geno did not respond, but he tilted his head as he looked to Taylor in solidarity, letting what he did not say send the message that it did not matter.

"Ok, I get that. I'm actually not surprised by Geno. I don't like you getting yourself involved with that business with my Uncles. You already know this. I got you though. Just don't ask me to go out to the country Taylor, I won't go. So, don't make me have to."

Taylor said nothing in response to what Vaughn had said. He just walked right up on him, and the two men shook hands and hugged on it without breaking eye contact during the exchange.

Langston, however, stood with the appearance of being confused by what just took place behind them both. Langston then looked over to Geno with an intense stare of intrigue. Then he spoke,

"I want Spank. Don't even front me either."

To this, Vaughn turned around with a sudden quickness, swooped into the personal space of his younger brother with explosive fury, and spoke loudly in his face.

"What are you talking about? I'm not letting you get involved in any of that Langston. Are you kidding me right now? Don't play yourself up here."

Challenged by the moment, Langston stood motionless, sucking his teeth momentarily as he seemed ready to strike his brother where he stood.

"Well, it's definitely happening. You can't stop me. I'm a grown mother fuckin' man Vaughn. You're really playing yourself, getting all in my face too. I'm going to overlook that because I know that you're just concerned. I don't have a choice. This total mess has been eating away at my soul since I was a freaking baby. This is my next move. Whether you like it. You just need to support me on this bruh. Straight like that."

Both Geno and Taylor both blew sighs of relief that the sudden disagreement settled as nicely as it did. Vaughn, however, uncharacteristically rattled with his younger brother's challenging demeanor. Vaughn was a man of integrity, and his over protecting impulses took over his better judgement for that moment. He recognized Langston was indeed a grown man now. He had no right to challenge him or place him in that position. He also did not want to relinquish his ability to protect and monitor most of his younger brother's comings and goings. He also knew that the day was coming where doing so would become less and less possible. That day had obviously come.

As the four men stood in the room, each in their own moment of revelation, there was motionless silence. Then suddenly the door burst open and in came Spunk, Poot, and Ox speaking loudly amongst each other, carrying, and eating their meals on plates. Once in the room, Spunk stopped short once he noticed the appearance of tension in the room and how the vibe had changed since they left. Ox just could prevent himself from running into him from behind, and so did Poot, who had been trailing in the rear.

"Nah, Vaughn, we are not killing the party this early man. Y'all got to get this thing back to the right energy in here. What the hell y'all got going on, anyway?"

Yelled out Spunk. Then Thomas continued,

"Geno, what the hell happened here? We can't even grab some food man? For real?"

At this, both Taylor and Geno looked in the direction where

Thomas stood, and Taylor remarked,

"We were just speaking about my decision to take on some additional work from Delegate Fortune. What we briefly discussed earlier this afternoon. Vaughn wasn't pleased, and Langston was hungry to get in on the ground floor. Vaughn is also displeased with that more than anything right now. Which is to be expected? That about sums it all up there. Please come on in, eat your food, and have some drinks. I want to go over the surface of what this will look like for us all in so many ways in the upcoming months regarding how we will rearrange personnel to accommodate for this shift in activity."

Taylor's Tone was light, yet commanding all the same for the attention of the moment. Vaughn was still contemplating how to make right with Langston for having that off display of public disrespect. While ironically enough Langston stands next to Geno and Taylor now, internally struggling with achieving full focus on what Taylor was speaking on while fighting off the strong distraction of dealing with the embarrassment that his older brother caused him by slighting his adult ability to stand on his own.

Geno, Vincent, and Thomas had been eagerly awaiting this additional information from the original announcement that afternoon, albeit brief. So, as Taylor continued to speak on how their people were to be reallocated and used, he also speaks on the need to have a follow-up meeting to this one in a more secure location. This was a necessity because of the sensitive nature of their operation and that of his idea to delve deeper into what he perceived would entail the work furnished to him from his Uncle.

So, with that, since he had the attention of the room, he gave the floor to Vaughn. Since it was Vaughn that summoned them all there, he felt it was right to not monopolize the moment. Not completely in his right focus, Vaughn walked over to the center of the room as Taylor returned to the seat from which he had eaten his meal from. After an uncomfortable moment of silence that was not totally uncommon from Vaughn, but his preoccupied demeanor was different and visibly obvious to the crew who also grew up alongside him, under his guidance. All the men in this room looked to Vaughn frequently in admiration for his stand-up guy personality. Langston finding solace in his brothers clearly recognizable consternation, stood up himself, and walked over to Vaughn and stood to the side of his brother, putting his hands on his shoulders, as he started to briefly rub his brother's shoulders to support whatever he had to say.

Consoled by this, Vaughn spoke;

"Initially, I called all of you here to discreetly take a moment amongst ourselves to just celebrate one of our own. I've watched each of you grow from silly little boys, into serious grown men. None of this without a collection of setbacks that taught each of us as we endured through them... who we were before the difficulty, and who we became after dealing with the adversity. Whether those situations found any of us respectively in victory, or momentarily swallowed in defeat. I've stood on the sidelines and in the trenches with all of you with grit, resiliency, and admiration for my younger brothers in arms."

"I just wanted to take the time to soak this moment in like the family we are and always will be regardless of what tomorrow has in store for us. Salute"

After Vaughn finished speaking, the entire room stood silent. Vaughn had walked to the door in their silence, opened the door, and called for a hostess to bring some bottles of champagne into the room. Once the bottles arrived, the men gathered together with bottles of Armand de Brignac Brut Gold, in each of their hands as they went without flutes for this occasion. Each man pointed their bottle to the ceiling as they each bellowed sporadic sentiments of elation. before they all took long swigs from their bottles. Just as they finished doing so, the door opened again. This time it was Khaleel entering the room, holding a similar bottle of his own. He walked right up to Taylor, one of his three nephews in the room. Once alongside him, Khaleel put his arm around Taylor and spoke into his ear since that was the only way to ensure what he was saying would be heard with all the commotion in the room at that moment.

"Taylor-Made! My Man Spank. Another chapter completes, and the story gets more interesting with each turning page nephew. My Sister, your beloved mother would have been immensely proud on this day without question. I am so proud of the man I've seen you turn into. I know you aint about to stop this train here, so we will have to definitely link up at a later date so I can pick your mind for the trailer to the next season of the Taylor Fortune Show."

Khaleel playfully and respectfully provoked his nephew as he has always had done. Nothing menacing or malicious, but drawing his beloved nephew's attention to things here and there. With Taylor, his Oldest sister's only son living with his brother-in-law primarily Khaleel wanted to ensure that he imparted some of that Proffit family mentality and understanding into him whenever possible. In this situation, how he went about doing this was to continue to poke small jabs at Taylor about his more visible lifestyle choices in comparison to himself.

Knowing that Taylor had some disdain for having the spotlight on him in most situations, if not internally all. Taylor was far from a true introvert, yet he just wasn't fond of his awareness of historical moments where successful enterprising individuals such as himself stepped into that light their corresponding businesses suffered significantly as a result. His uncle was well aware of this concern his nephew fostered. This comment was just more of the same for the two of them. Taylor, upon hearing this smirked deeply as he took a next swig from his bottle. In kind, traditionally consistent with this banter between the two, Taylor took great joy in his Uncle's timing. Realizing that he could get double the shock of his recent developments by sharing the initial news of his decision to take on some work in connection to his Uncle Demetrius's extra-curricular activities.

"Oh yeah Uncle K."

Tylor began his words to his uncle as he leaned into his shoulder to finish speaking directly into his uncle's ear to ensure what he was about to say was heard completely.

"Now that my calendar is opening up wider due to no longer having to attend the University, I will be taking some time to work closer with my Father and Uncle on some things here in the States."

Khaleel too stood back away from Taylor quickly as he said this as did Vaughn earlier. in Shock and sudden frustration and disbelief,

Khaleel sucked his teeth then moaned out to his nephew, "Rasclaat!"

"Why are you playing with me?"

Khaleel, sucking his teeth again, walked backwards in disapproval, facing Taylor as he approached Vaughn as Taylor watched him do so with a smirk on his face. Seeming to relish in his disapproval slightly. Their relationship consists of more similar moments between the two of them. With just Langston remaining at his side, Taylor turned to him with a noticeable anticipation as he started to ascertain the seriousness of his younger cousin.

"So, are you serious? Or were you just pissing Vaughn off?"

"I am dead ass serious T" was Langston's' quick and stern response.

"Dead, Ass, Serious. How do we get this started? That is the thing that I need to know, cousin."

Taylor stood back, and took a second look at his cousin with some concern as he knew that Langston was a developing hot head that had only 2 switches in his gearbox. Calm collected, to straight crazy. Taylor was well aware of how this move would enhance these traits in his younger and slightly dissociated cousin. He also was aware that once Langston had made his mind up about something, that he was certainly going to see it through to its end.

What that end looked like at the moment was an alarming thought, but what Taylor honestly knew that he did not have was the time available to talk him out of it, and handle his own full plate.

He also knew that at least in him deciding to do so, that he would have a right hand that he could definitely trust while molding at the same time in more than a few areas where his cousin had been needing some influence. Hopefully this opportunity would produce other opportunities to do just that.

Taylor placed his hand firmly on Langston's shoulder as he peered into his cousin's eyes...

"Then that's what it is then. We take this journey together. I totally identify with what I can only imagine to be part of your motivation to get in on this move. Even with that potentially being the case, and despite how that must be a potent incentive for many impulses to rise to the top of your thoughts and as a result your choices. This move is primarily my move. So, considering I can relate to these provocations I will need you to trust me with how we proceed. When it's appropriate for you to go handle business the way you see fit,

I will gladly let you know, but until that time. You need to know and completely understand that before I give you the green light to roll with me in this operation, we have to be in complete agreement here. Nothing less."

Langston, forebodingly never changed his disposition, and continued to glare intensely into Taylor's eyes with a blank unwavering expression of acceptance in all of what he had said to him. Slightly concerned with this, Taylor smirked at his cousin barely, and Put his arm all the way around his shoulder and reach around with his other arm to shake his hand as he spoke to him again,

"So, it begins. We will handle all of that business before we finish too. Just work with me cuz. Work with me"

The two men then looked about the room at the other six men all engaged in their own assortment of communication. Taylor released his grip around Langston's shoulders as he began to make his way towards the wall where Geno and Poot were standing speaking with Spunk, while Langston unbothered nor reluctant began to walk toward his Uncle and his older brother.

"Let's enjoy the time we have tonight for this sort of thing while we can."

Taylor uttered faintly but clearly as they momentarily parted ways... Langston had a bottle, but it was not of champagne. He had a smaller bottle of Fireball Whiskey in his hand, draped inside of a crisply creased paper bag. The two sides of the room eventually brought it together as Ramone, the business partner of Vivian came through the door with sparkles over a new set of champagne bottles and the remarkable women toting them behind him.

"I know you ain't about all this Taylor, but CONGRATULATIONS

TO YOU MY BROTHER! Everyone is proud of what you've done in such a short time. Enjoy the drinks, and the company. Vivian has some wings heading in also just to keep y'all on point."

Ramone then approached Khaleel, who was a close associate of his, and they conversed amid the ensuing festivities. Much enjoyment took place that evening for all the men.

CHAPTER 6

"Manila Envelope"

The next morning at approximately six forty-five, the city was just receiving the long, extending reach of the sun's rays. So blindly potent that the view from Taylor's loft was overcome by it. As the slew of digital gadgetry chimed to the exact time of six forty-five televisions automatically turned on, coffee pots brewed, and the air handler administered to the climate. Even the shower was preparing for the shower, just as Taylor preferred it. We find Taylor standing close to his rather large balcony window in the bedroom with three women of voluptuous shaped sprawled out unconscious in random arrangement over his noticeably large

California king-size bed. As three different, but all efficiently silent rhumba like devices maneuvered about the residence. Taylor walked to his kitchen, in what appeared to be his usual poised disposition. Still wearing no clothes from the endeavors of the hours extending after his departure from the lounge.

While in the kitchen, he reached for one of his cabinet doors, opened it slowly as he moved throughout his space in a contemplative zone. He grabbed a coffee mug after some thoughts on which one. Once he had his Mug for the morning, he then closed the cabinet door back, and headed towards the countertop where his coffee machine had been brewing his favorite brand of coffee. After he poured a healthy amount into his cup, he turned to the refrigerator and took a small bottle of flavored creme out. Once his coffee was customized for his pallet, Taylor used the handset in the docking station and made a call.

"Javier? Buenos dias mi gente,"

"Si, necesito el desayuno para las seis de Esta mañana.

¿puedes venir ahora?"

Once his request was graciously accepted, Taylor nimbly grabbed his coffee mug, as he enthusiastically walked back to his bedroom, into his closet while passing by the three beautiful women draped across his bed again. This time he doubled back to enjoy the view and experienced some nostalgia as he marveled in each of the lady's remarkable gorgeousness before he continued into his walkin closet, which was quite large and lacking any detail.

It was through the walk-in closet that led to his master bath suite. With the shower completely ready for the preferred water temperature, ideal to Taylor's taste, Taylor entered the lavishly tiled structure and bathed for nearly fifteen minutes. After his shower, Taylor walked through his Closet collecting his underwear from where they had been stored, an undershirt, a pair of socks before he sat on the handcrafted wooden bench that laid against one wall, across from the mirror and raised a section of flooring in front of the mirror.

Once he had those items on, he began looking through some binders that showcased his wardrobe, including their location in the closet. His decorator had implemented this feature for him per Taylor's request to better navigate through his clothing in moments such as this.

Now fully dressed, Taylor walked up to his jewelry cabinet. After a moment taken to further consider his choice, Taylor reached in, grabbed a watch, a medium-sized gold chain, a set of cufflinks, and a gold pinky ring. Walking back into the bedroom as he was putting the jewelry on the three women were moving and become more awake. One spoke out for Taylor, which prompted the other two to turn and watch for his reaction.

"Good Morning Baby! (flirtatious giggling) whatever that is cooking smells absolutely delicious. Is that for us? Mmm mmm."

Taylor turned towards the bed where they laid, as he straightened his French cuffs into the cufflinks. Shared a smile as he spoke to them all.

"Yes, my chef came in just for the three of you. Made something special per my request. So please enjoy every bit. I am famished myself from the three of you but have meetings I may not already make so I have to run. I have three drivers waiting for you all down in the lobby, waiting to take you anywhere you desire. If you need to be in another state, let the driver know, and he has those accommodations as well already prepared. I will be out of the city for a week when I return hopefully, we can find time for one another."

Taylor then crawled on the edge of the bed as the women crawled in response towards him for some farewell embraces. After a few moments of the women working to entice Taylor back into the sheets, and back out of his clothes, he snickered and stepped back off the bed's edge as he lingered in ceasing to French Kiss each of the women very much in his personal space at the moment.

"You also smell delicious Hunny"

Remarked one woman, as she exaggerated the usage of her tongue and mouth while slowly enunciating her words.

Taylor did pause with the stunning beauty that momentarily froze his resistance as she purposefully provoked his enticement with her seductive utterance. The other two women also chimed in utilizing the same tactics,

"Yeah baby, you smell appetizing."

"Oh yes baby, at least come back so I can have one more whiff of you."

Both women spoke with mischievous smirks, accompanied by innocently batting eyes. Successfully aroused, but unsuccessfully tempted, Taylor blew some kisses to women as he signed in regret as he departed the room. As Taylor walked through the kitchen, Javier had already had a small burrito prepared the way he likes to be with the wrapper peeled back, ready to be consumed, as he walked through the kitchen. As the two men elbow bumped one another, Taylor also slipped him a somewhat thick to about an inch folded manilla envelope, wrapped in a rubber band. Upon the complete exchange of the envelope, Javier and Taylor shared brief eye contact as acceptance that the handoff was received and appreciated. Taylor left the loft into the elevator where Jonathan greeted him.

As the doors shut, the elevator awaited instructions from the operator to continue, Jonathan and Taylor saluted each other.

Once the elevator made its descent to the lobby, Taylor had told Jonathan to make sure he had a productive day. He also reminded him to keep an eye open for things he knew he'd want to be aware of throughout the shift he was working.

Jonathan assured him this was already the case.

Taylor departed the elevator cabin onto the parking deck, on his way to the garage. He did not want to wait in the lobby for having the valet retrieve his vehicle. So, he went and grabbed the keys from the valet station on the parking deck and went directly to his car, pulling out onto the construction exit to the building. As Taylor sped along through Columbia heights, taking an elongated route so he could come through Georgia Avenue and pass through his campus on the main strip, as he

was expecting making a rendezvous with an associate over there to pick up some items of moderate importance for later appointments in the day's itinerary. Almost at the exact moment he made the right on Georgia Avenue, he received a text message from Demetrius where he was hoping to meet with him for lunch this afternoon out and about though. Not at an establishment, but at a food cart somewhere he'll inform him about around the time they were to meet. Odd enough, but par for the course with his Uncle. Taylor pulled out his smart mobile device and opened its calendar app to see where he could expect to find himself around the part of his itinerary that afternoon. Taylor sent a short text back to his Uncle,

"Hey Unc, I will be close to Lincoln Park around lunch. Can you try to find something near there to meet up for me, please?" His Uncle quickly responded, "Not a problem. There are a few locations in that area we already frequent, so not a problem, nephew."

Taylor put his phone back on its dock, and continued to make his way to Girard Street, where he made that left onto the one way. As Girard turned into sixth and Taylor could see the Green Stadium, he slowed much of the way down to a coast rate of progress as he continued on until sixth now turned into Fairmont, where he pulled off to the side of the curb along the curve a way past the fire hydrant.

Shortly after his arrival, along the stone flower bed from down the staircase, arose an individual who walked inconspicuously to the parked vehicle, and handed Taylor two wrapped and folded manilla envelopes. Then as smooth as these items were inserted carefully into the discreetly extended a hand out of the window of that vehicle, that indescribable individual walked off and instantly blended back into the bustling collegiate thoroughfare by Stadium. From there, Taylor headed towards Minnesota Avenue to meet up, or more like pop up on Vaughn. With his intention to follow up with Vaughn so he can prepare him to coordinate with Spunk and Geno, who were his Captains regarding the operation. Confident in their knowledge of the operation, and ability to walk him through what will be needed of him. What he needed to speak to him directly about was the general manner in which he needed him to conduct business. Taylor knew their difference in interpersonal approach was the key issue to his capability to keep things out of chaos and running smoothly.

Taylor also respected the burden he would undertake to even assist him in this way. Vaughn had his own operation in the City. He started with just a few of his original friends, and with the tutelage of his former Guardian, and Uncle Khaleel, he ran a large part of his Uncle's trade on their end of the city. So, his role is more a show of solidarity and support in appearance for his captains who didn't have the muscle that Vaughn and Khaleel had.

Once Taylor turned onto Minnesota Ave and continued to drive a few blocks east bound until he veered to his right on R street. He received a text from Vaughn coincidentally,

"Yooo."

Taylor hit him back,

"Yooo."

Vaugh then gave Taylor directions on where they would meet.

"Iight, turn right on Twenty-Second, and then pull up on the corner of Twenty-Second and Ridge."

Taylor followed his instructions, then discreetly pulled up on the corner under one of its larger trees. As he did this, a metallic grey late model SUV pulled up alongside his vehicle and Vaughn stepped out quickly, shutting the door behind him, then entered the vehicle with his cousin.

"What's up, cuzzo? What's on your mind. Not surprised you're out and about this morning. I think we all left preoccupied last night."

"Yeah, I appreciate the sendoff. It was a hard-fought mission that I am happy had ended when it did. I definitely will miss having that direct connection to the pulse of the student body, and all that came with that. For sure." Taylor responded.

"Yeah, that's what I was thinking about really as I had been racking my brain trying to figure out why you got this ambition to get involved in all that mess. Then that very fact hit me square on the headman. Eventually the influence you've built has to change along with your degree of professional success. I know you're not going to run for any office, but I also know you still want that reach and influence of some of those offices, like Uncle D." Taylor sank back in his seat in appreciation for the tone, and the manner in which his cousin was communicating his philosophies. He had to admit that his cousin knew him well enough to realize he was onto something as he continued to speak.

"So, that's why I changed my mind and attitude on the subject. Not to mention, I also hope that at the end of that hallway you bring me back the hands of the men responsible for the killing of my parents. That brings me to my next point. Langston. I

know he's been itching to do something, anything to feel like he hasn't just forgotten or let what happened go. I figured that after some reflection that he's better off moving under your watch than accidentally snapping out here on one of these clowns."

Again, Taylor could only provide facial expressions of positive acknowledgement as he found himself in agreement with what Vaughn was saying. He was actually relieved that he led off with all of this because he was just going to waste time trying to get where he already was if he had led. Then, as Vaughn gauged how Taylor's quietness was going to say, Taylor saw this opportunity and he spoke,

"You've covered a lot of ground quick, and accurately. I agree with what you're saying. We are seeing the same board right now. The next set of potential moves need to be seen and understood by us both as well. We need to understand why they are the foundation of the choices to make pending unforeseen circumstances that we know will arise and create opportunities for improvisation. I'm relieved, I was certain that getting you here was going to require more of me trying to bring you to where you've already brought yourself. I am in awe of you right now, and you already know I try not to boost that big ass head of yours up any more than it already is."

Taylor spoke with sincerity and finished with a joke for his ever developing cousin. With the two of them now seeing things along the same lines regarding what was at stake, Taylor took the time to mention some of his concerns.

"I know that with what you have going on, you need to be stern and ruthless. What I am putting you on to is different. Although your presence is to nonverbally communicate the ability, show teeth or possess teeth that are obviously in the mouth, without having to actually bite let alone devour a person. The threat is in the ability. The power is in preventing such an outcome without ever having to allude to the outcome. Some may not follow this format. Geno or Spunk knows who these characters are. We have plans on bringing them into irrefutable compliance in due time. Their false security in their current pathways is what we want to take place just as it is. I just need you to lead by just being you. Just being there is enough. My guys will show how we have this sewn up."

It was now Vaughn who was brought to a shockingly speechless position, as he sat silent with an expression of cogitation across his countenance. He knew what he was saying had hit home in more than a few ways. It was the ugly truth of the matter of his endeavors. He accepted what his younger cousin had said.

Expected him for saying it additionally.

Taylor and Vaughn sat back and looked at one another with increased respect and growing admiration for their growth as men. Vaughn pulled out his mobile device and sent a quick text.

moments later, a different SUV pulled up from the next corner and Vaughn opened his door to get out. Before he departed, he gave Taylor some dap and spoke, "Say less. We will handle that when the time comes. By the way, you won't believe me but it was actually Uncle K who brought my thinking around."

Taylor quickly spoke back,

"Hell no! that I wouldn't normally believe, but what you are not is a liar, so wow! We're all leveling up out here!"

"Yeah, I knew that was gonna blow your mind right there!" Vaughn closed the door and then vanished into the streets as he jumped into the next SUV and it shot off the block.

Now with that prematurely handled better than expected, Taylor pulled off from the curb, and sped off down Ridge until he hit Nineteenth, and worked his way towards T street. He made a stop to see an associate at the body shop off good hope before he doubled back up to Minnesota where he took that up to Pennsylvania Avenue, so he could cross the Sousa Bridge and continue on that road to eleventh, which would take him right to his meeting hopefully near Lincoln park with Demetrius in just enough time to spare before he was expecting his Uncle to hit him up with the exact location of the meetup. Taylor encountered some traffic as he approached the Sousa, but got across in a timely manner all the same considering the time of day he was making the trip.

As he reached eleventh and turned, he glanced at his watch and realized he had some free time before he could expect a communication from his Uncle so he parked along East Capitol street where he had gained a brownstone a few years back. The brownstone was his initial residence before the move to the loft. While he still possessed it, he converted it into an office for the staff he had working around the immediate area. The coincidence served him well.

With several other locations spread throughout the city facilitating similar purposes, Taylor and his crew had the foundation to really take advantage of what an alliance with the political force that came with Delegate Fortune represented. Taylor and his captains knew well that what this meant was that clients that typically required Taylor's touch would have to now become their clients. Without leaving them feeling less valued or heard when they came with problems to be solved, they collectively understood that it will require each of their games to completely step up and further develop in order to consume all that was potentially coming their way.

As Taylor scoped into the park with piercing vision, he walked down the sidewalk along the string of the brownstones along the street. When he arrived at the location of his brownstone, he jogged up its staircase and reach for the doorknob, then turned it as the door opened. Since the entire Brownstone had belonged to him, the entire building was basically used as one connected office.

The top floor was reserved as a residence if people needed to stay over and work late. Taylor ran a twenty-four-hour operation, so he had several shifts of people coming and going because he definitely did not encourage his people to become burnt out. The major activity however was handed on the second floor. So that's where Taylor was headed to. As he jogged up the staircase and onto the second floor, he saw the familiar faces of his team. Greeted on sight, he eventually got to the room used as the primary office. Within it was Vincent, occasionally referred to as Ox amongst the crew and one of their Lieutenants discussing matters. They had the office working to prepare for the transition looming under the expected changes coming down the pipe.

With all of his satellites over the city, Taylor was a marvel to his team on all levels because he took the time to walk into each location at least once if not twice a week besides his multitude of meetings he took in the streets, using the parks and their benches for a five-minute conversation here, a ten-minute meeting over there, etc.

Thriving in taking advantage of his youth and doing more with more than usually doing so with less sleep than one would think he was getting. Despite learning from the master of doing less with more, the esteemed Delegate Fortune.

Whom he had been setting up to meet with next. After a very brief status report from Vincent, Taylor, satisfied with the production and demeanor of the office's energy level, then hiked back down the stairs. Before he did, he stated to Vincent,

"Ox, I have a meeting across the street in the park with my Uncle about the change. Hit me on the hip if you make it to having someone heading over to see my youngin on campus later." While Taylor was midway down the staircase, he got the text he'd been waiting for.

"Meet me on the north side of the park in about fifteen minutes across from the playground by the statues. There is a stone pier that stretches out long enough for us both. I'll bring a few burritos like you like them. If you're down with that. I don't know if you're hungry or not, let me know."

"Sure."

Taylor texted back. He left the vehicle where it had been parked and instead made his way on foot into the park. Coming from the opposite side of the designated spot in the park where he was told the meetup would occur, he afforded himself to pay closer attention as he drew nearer to the current inhabitants already inside the park. Constantly seeking a heightened sense of awareness, Taylor observed the people and their overall mannerisms as he passed by some, and noticed others from a distance as he navigated his way to the location discussed. Taylor arrived at the bench and took his seat, as he sat there continuing to look around, sure enough he saw the motorcade pulled up to the curb in typical Delegate Fortune fashion. As the protection specialists moved around his vehicle to prepare for Demetrius's departure from his SUV, Taylor remained observant of his overall surroundings as his surroundings grew astonished with the sudden spectacle unraveling with quickness before their eyes. With the SUV not exactly far from the bench in which Taylor had been sitting, and Demetrius still in mid approach to find his place on the bench. The two men exchanged eye contact. There was some elation in both of their eyes as they laid eyes on one another. Taylor stood up and approached his Uncle with a handshake.

"Uncle D!"

"Taylor made!"

There was then a brief embrace before the two of them sat down together on the bench. Demetrius took a moment, looking over his nephew as he preparing to speak.

"What is paramount Taylor for you to understand most thoroughly here is that despite the urgency of the climate, and the lack of time in which to walk you through all the relative information surrounding the situations at play I want to bring you into the fold. Mostly, this decision to bring you in has come with hesitation and debate between me and your father.

The opportunity is profound. There are countless positive benefits that can be easily identifiable from your participation, and there are many additional vulnerabilities that are surely not as positive.

They are negative and in that I am referring to life threatening. Without question, the moment you officially commit to anything we have going which will require you to involve yourself in a physical present manner. This can be as simple as being in a particular place, looking into situations, asking questions, and such things will permanently tether you to this organization we represent and its operations.

This commitment will change your life, and as you perform more work on the various assignments thrown your way, it

will consequently add an unparalleled opportunity for you in areas you may never even had expected to access, let alone have the network we have available to grow your total outlook exponentially in a most expedient time frame. You will need to appreciate the significance of this challenge.

Because immediately upon doing so, the world as you have known it will instantly change for you in every imaginable way. What you need to determine and then decide is whether that this path is one you can commit to. I will not sugarcoat this for you. When my brother, your father, made this choice, he was very gung-ho and eager to earn his bones in the field.

In Doing so he racked up a rather incendiary profile. The ultimate cost of that profile that he got brought a heavy burden upon us all. It was in relation to this profile and the allure of being wanted by countless international hitmen that the fight followed his name here to DC and stole with it the lives of his Wife, your mother and her sister and husband all in one catastrophic evening none of us will ever be able to forget, let alone fully recover from."

Taylor sat shocked and momentarily in bewilderment as he listened to his Uncle. Almost in disbelief, he grew quite motivated to follow this thread even further into the abyss, knowing that somewhere within this series of endeavors he will ultimately be rewarded with the chance to avenge the murder of his mother, Aunt, and Uncle. For the first time in slightly over twenty years since that disastrous night, He found a peaceable sensation growing within him now knowing that such an opportunity to vindicate his fallen mother was becoming something that was realistic and growing real as he continued to entertain the words spoken to him through his Uncle. While slightly distracted by the voice of concern and betrayal, why he was never told until now that the motives behind the murder of his mother had been known by either his father or uncle all this time. Feeling somewhat betrayed that this was something he had wished to have been told over the course of all that time in between that irreversible moment in his youth to now. More disappointed than angered, seeing that it was just the two of them living under the same roof for years and countless one-on-one conversations shared during that time span.

Taylor, saturated with curiosity, could no longer remain silent with his uncle on the many pressing matters swirling through his mind. Speaking, "Uncle D, I ain't trying to trip over the details of what happened to my mother, but you've known all this apparently for so long. How come I am just now being told what you seem to know already."

Taylor started again quickly with agitation before Demetrius had the chance to frame his mouth to speak.

"What, you didn't think I could handle any of that? Man, Uncle that's foul that you're just sharing that with me after all these years!"

Demetrius did Grimace slightly, as he sat quietly still beside his nephew. With his head now shifting upwards with his focus on the clouds above, Demetrius inhaled a rather pronounced and deep breath. One inhaled, he then blew out the air as his cheeks deflated, leaving his lips to quiver as the air rushed through them.

Finally, Demetrius responded to an eagerly expecting Taylor.

"After those events that horrified us all transpired, we simply thought it best to watch how the following months went. If there were excessive questions, we would have strived to provide an appropriate response. However, I kept you preoccupied in other endeavors that enticed your developmental curiosity in positive directions. Or so we thought so and knowing that with not much information on the attack in our possession, and the individuals responsible additionally not fully known to either of us, we did not see the benefit in adding insult to injury in keeping you and your cousins in that loop of developing information. As time continued to speed along, and your remarkable adaptation to the curriculum and surroundings my home provided to you we decided it was in your best interest to hold off on bringing that subject up again hoping for many years you would not bring up those questions, forcing us to speak directly on it. Especially during the years when much of the information we now have, wasn't available to us during that time."

Taylor's expression simmered down. He expected nothing but the absolute best responses from his Uncle because his Uncle typically had some of the best and more thought-out responses to questions and the situations surrounding them. A talent well developed by his time serving the public, and all that accompanies that role regarding responding to people wanting information he did not always have. He would respond to his inquisitors in such a manner where he nullified additional questions into the same subject. An art form he had remotely close to perfection, and it made him endearing to the press. Brought him into roles where he would be requested to speak on behalf of many committees (after formally being invited to join several for just that purpose). Taylor seemed to accept his response, as he understood the framework of the logic in his explanation. He turned to his Uncle and simply said with an abnormally humbled look on his face. "You made a good point. As a man I want to be involved, but I could understand I was just a kid. I do want to start this journey and in order to do so I need as much information that your able and willing to share with me so this commitment that I am making can be made with the most comprehension of what is entailed within it. I need for this to be a move Unc. You know me and you understand mostly how I approach life. Enough to understand what I am not about. Put me in a position to win my way if you have the influence in that, like you do everywhere else. I assume you do, because you want me to roll with you."

Demetrius was not overly surprised with his nephews' statement, or requests from within it. He had already envisioned his concerns roughly, and this input clarified where he was spot on target and shed light on a few items he could surely ensure would be implemented. Demetrius not only wanted this to work effectively, but he needed to give Taylor a better start in this than he could provide his brother when he started out- always in the corner of his mind lamented some regret towards the idea of if he had done so, perhaps the tragedy would have never occurred.

Preventing himself from becoming overrun with grief, and empathetic thoughts as to the realities of what could have been concerning the murder of Mrs. Dorothy, and how her absence could have easily bore an irreparable hole in Taylors's soul that no endeavor could properly repair. Demetrius then spoke again. "I will work hand in hand with you to implement a method of approach that will be tailored for you, and your success in the assignments I feel better suits your current set of skill sets and talents. In time under the direction I provide, to include the occasional guidance from your father when he becomes available, the areas that you may consider as less than strong suited areas of your abilities may give you cause to reevaluate yourself.

Possibly more than a few times you may find the need to re-assess and evaluate. First, you ought to know that your resume made this development possible for you in our eyes. It wasn't just that you actually created a strategically insulated network, that made you an extremely difficult candidate to attract any litigation or negative attention from any legitimate law enforcement agencies. You've obviously done well for yourself, young man, and it is the method in which you went about it that set your accomplishments in a light of their own for us both. Your decisiveness, and the energies you exhausted to keep your endeavors private and discreet. This alone was very impressive, so naturally once I noticed your dealings quite a few years ago I saw the invitation as an opportunity to monitor your comings and goings with a special circle of some of my trusted staff. Using them to maintain a special and significantly discreet veil of protection over you, to include the matters of business you dealt with. I did that then as I have continued to do even this day, so this moment we share now would be possible"

Taylor, now with more intrigue, responded. "To me, you represent the personification of power. The definition of true success, but honestly, I am still a young man, and more specifically

I facilitate a tiny purpose in a picture tremendously larger than myself regarding the dealings in the organization you and my father share affiliation with. One that has brought our family this wealth of blessings that I am a beneficiary to. I want in. Again, we just need to establish the how."

Demetrius, internally teeming with appreciation of the kind words bestowed upon him by his nephew, took a moment as he placed his hand briefly on the kneecap of his nephew. Then spoke once more, "So, follow me on this expedition that had been forged over centuries of obligation to a set of core principles and ideals. Fundamental values based upon the very ingredients of what was used to create the very constitution itself, by men who also participated in the nation's liberation we have come to know." Demetrius continued on, "Well the current climate leaves us already significantly behind on time and things have become increasingly hostile. This is why we are in dire need of your contribution. I am placing a significant amount of faith in your raw potential. Ther a few other things I will expose to you Before I must run off about my day, and leave you to yours. Something so serious, so irreversibly confidential and sacred, that I could not even tell you until we had officially consummated an understanding of the parameters of what we hold dear in this affiliation we consider most sacred. No matter what, you MUST trust me. You must commit yourself to follow my guidance through to the end. We will do this together regardless of what the situation may have you perceive to be reality or truth. You have never been what most would label a follower so I can imagine that these propositions of allegiance and secrecy might take you not only by surprise, but may very well leave you regrettably unwilling to go any further . . . this is to be understood. You are at this particular time free to do as you choose. Taylor, I see you've verbally committed to taking the next series of steps however, trust that above all else... We are family. A family that does not possess a history of weakness in times of action. Despite that being the norm in our current era. Therefore, when I ask you to trust your life with me, I am asking my brothers' son, My

Mother's Grandson to trust me. So, make no mistake about this, you could meet your death if you fail to stay vigilant or follow the guidance provided by not only me but of those, I have prepared you to study under to prepare you for what to expect and overcome during your time representing this

allegiance. Frankly your demise can be an eventuality at any given moment. The risk here is real and perpetual."

Taylor nodded his head in agreement, paused, then asked a question to his Uncle, "You have used the phrase 'We' an awful lot. Is this something new that I need to expect moving forward?" Demetrius shed a menacing grin, as he couldn't resist from looking away to prevent an all-out smile from burning across his face as he looked off towards his SUV and nodded.

At that moment, the other side of the SUV had its driver's side passenger door thrust open. As whoever was sitting in the vehicle all this time had been making their way around to the side where they could enter the park and approach them both, they began to speak strongly,

"We would and have always included me, Son."

Denard Fortune bellowed in his deep, sultry baritone. Taylor stood tall and unsuccessfully fought off emotion as he was beyond thankful to see his father again after a long absence from the area. Denard opened his arms as he continued to approach his brother and son. Taylor and Denard embrace strongly. after a powerful moment where they held one another like the grown son and Proud father would be expected to if they were constantly in each other's presence. This moment had heightened this sentiment, as the two men had not laid eyes on one another for about two-anda-half years.

Denard spoke again as he pulled back softly from their embrace to gaze upon his son and marvel in the acknowledgement of his growth and maturation from the last time, he could set eyes upon his son.

"We will have plenty of time this evening at your Uncle's home to get caught up on the last two years. I managed to convince at great expense of my own that tonight's meal will just be the three of us."

Then just as smoothly as he arrived and started to speak, so it was as smoothly he ceased to speak, re-entered the SUV and departed. His security detail operated in almost reverse as they precisely moved him from the bench to his car door with Denard following suit. Abruptly it was all over, almost as if it never took place despite a slight screech from the tires pulling off sternly from the curb down East Capital west bound towards eleventh street, where the string of SUV's sped off veering left onto Massachusetts Avenue out of sight.

CHAPTER 7

"Awakening"

Immediately after the convoy of the esteemed Delegate's departure, a strong stench of burnt rubber filled the air around the immediate area of where they initially pulled off with haste from the curb. Taylor returned to his seat on the bench as thy sped off, and he had remained seated there up against the backrest of the bench in a mild stupor. At this point Taylor was confronted with not just having to face a demon from deep within, but also of years past. For on the one hand, he still admired his often absent, but extremely bold and brave father.

While also having to acknowledge and accept that his uncle was correct in that somewhere within there was still a significant part of him that wanted to pursue their mysterious endeavors, so the two could finally share something, and give them a bond he'd desired all his life. Where on the other hand, himself, along with the collaboration and diligence of his team, who started as boys and grew to be men together. Battle tested and proven amongst one another, stood side by side in the creation of a truly remarkable enterprise that could very well outlive them all if properly operated.

As Taylor sat, he pondered the enigmatic components of his conundrum in the pursuit of formulating an effective strategy that would produce an efficacious outcome. Although finding some reassurance in the words of his Uncle, and the rapid ongoing internal development of a myriad of potential contingency plans to ensure his confidence in his capability to find victory against the possible contradistinctive entities he'd be facing. While also accepting that how these entities would do him the honor of introducing themselves. Having already been pressed for time, he signaled his people to get his itinerary updated, and forwarded to him in consideration of the time he had remaining to handle his more pressing matters of his day before the typical close of business in the area sprung upon them.

His data was sent to his mobile device through the designated secured process in addition to the interface integrated in his vehicle. Taylor had the computer science department at Howard and some of its highest performing students whom he had other dealings with in regards to his extracurricular enterprise to develop a network for his vehicles to share secured data with his network that connected his offices throughout the region. He then instructed them to send a message he drafted to both Vaughn and Colin. Then, he sent an additional message to his team, Vaughn, and Langston informing the team there was an urgent need to meet with pertinent information and new developments to discuss.

With the meeting set, Taylor maneuvered to his residence to change his clothes, because he wanted to get some time at his gym before the meeting. He was aggressively motivated to get in an impactful workout. So, Taylor had changed into his workout attire, and had made it to the gym on a lower level in the building. As he began his exercise routine it began with his arms and shoulders, all that was on his mind was being good enough to step it up in every imaginable and even perhaps unimaginable ways to him. He was mostly in the dark regarding what these new endeavors would bring into his life, but he knew that in order to have the best shot at whatever victory looked like in this.

This will require his physical fitness to be taken much further than where it currently stood. His entire understanding of fitness was surely about to be obliterated, and significantly enhanced if he was going to become a formidable member of this new team, he still knew very little about it. Taylor interrogated himself, pulling no punches as he progressed into his workout.

"Will I be physically able to make this all work, and keep myself safe from death and serious injury? What if what this will require of me prove to be more than I am prepared for? What if I fail?"

Of course, these thoughts pushed him to frustration, and then to aggression, which was ideal for his workout. Ultimately opening his eyes to the reality of his intended endeavors, and how failure equated to death. and how death was quite final.

"will it be worth that level of risk?"

Getting more of an intensified workout as he pondered, he considered that with already having a great many things going for him, more than most had at his age. Inspired by genuine curiosity. Taylor continued to ponder whether or not the potential for complacency concerned him enough to disregard the possibility of becoming ungrateful of his successes, or somehow reckless enough in the appreciation or better yet the proper valuation of his own life in the pursuit of a broadening bond, and relationship with his often estranged father, that he'd jeopardize his own life to pursue the very possibility of an opportunity to avenge his mother while not to mention exponentially expanding his operations?

With the addition of each repetition and its compounding set count, his thoughts expanded beyond the acceptance aspect, and honed into perhaps the lack of full understanding of why he still generated these thoughts that so impactfully compelled him to consider embarking on this quest. The urge and motivation to do so was increasing within him most vigorously as he became deeper entranced into both his regimen, as well as the playlist selected for the sole purpose of inducing extreme diligence, and an intensified appetite for heightened performance.

After he concluded the workout of his arms, shoulders and back, Taylor ran for about a half an hour at his fastest speed until he was forced to stop from utter exhaustion. With every fourth thrust of his knees, up and forward he began to take his thoughts back to the bigger picture of tasking out how the most efficient strategy would play out, contingencies, and how to insulate not only his success, but the success of his team. Most importantly, due to the demonstrated history he was aware of in relation to the collateral damage that seemed to follow his father everywhere he went in

one manner or another since the loss of his Mother, and its associated volatility complicated the success of this new objective.

By this time his workout was all but complete. Taylor sat laid back in the hot tub playing chess with an Artificially intelligent opponent via his hands-free Bluetooth microphone headset, communicating his moves through voice command. He simply had to speak the piece name and intended square location he planned to move on the board into the microphone.

"Mahogany Queen to 'G5'."

Taylor spoke softly into his microphone piece.

Relaxed, yet focused in his thoughts, he contemplated further on the larger picture at play. Two brief games of chess later and he finished undefeated. After the hot tub, Taylor then left from there back home to his personal shower he had set by remote to be awaiting his arrival at his desired settings. His routine when he'd hit the gym. Once showered and dressed, he grabbed something from his fridge to eat, then departed into the elevator again to handle the remaining business of his day with enhanced focus and recognition before he tended to the business at hand that evening first with his team regarding his decision, then following up with his Father and Uncle to close out his night.

These thoughts swirled through his mind as he made his way to the parking deck. He passed off an envelope to Jonathon discreetly in passing as he exited the elevator onto the parking deck level. As Taylor travelled out of the parking area of the building out into the city, he used voice commands to engage his integrated mobile device. He then placed a call to Chairman Vanessa Willoughby, whom he had previously met with to discuss a need she had for him to address for her, emphasizing on a successful outcome. Although initially he was not fully informed as to what this need entailed.

The brief description of the task sounded familiar to what his Uncle had presented to him a few days ago, and her proposition came oddly before that. So, the timing was good for him to follow up with her, and take the next step into providing her his services in her dilemma. So, Taylor called her and asked to meet with her near her office.

"Thank you for reaching out to Chairman Willoughby, our two term Congresswoman representing Texans every day of the tenth district fighting and winning over twelve years for the great people in or community"

The administrative assistant spoke,

"Yes, Good afternoon. I was returning a call to the

Congresswoman. Is she available?"

"Good afternoon, Mr. Fortune, I know she was expecting your call. I will see if I can connect your call if you do not mind being placed on a brief hold?"

Then a slight pause in the line before the soothing jazz chimed across the speaker. After a few minutes of music, it came to an offbeat, abrupt end.

"Hello Mr. Fortune? Are you still on the line?"

"Yes."

"Well, Mr. Fortune, I will connect your call now ok?"

"Thank you. Have a great rest of your day and a hopefully a relaxing evening if that is what you want."

"Thank you, I will try. You have a great evening yourself..."

The phone again went silent for a second before ringing again.

"Good afternoon Taylor! I hope you have reconsidered my request and have a favorable response for me?"

"I actually have reconsidered. Yes. Can you have the details brought over to me in about thirty minutes at the south side of the park on D street and Second Street? I will be on the bench across from the parking meter."

"Done. Thank you for taking the time to look into this for me. I will be most grateful for your successful closure of these matters." Both lines simultaneously disconnected. As Taylor made a few additional calls before actually making his way over to the designated meeting location, his mind worked a little harder and his focus became clearer.

Taylor made it near the location, parking his vehicle across the street in the large parking lot behind the State Capitol Police headquarters. He then made his way to the park nonchalantly, picking up a newspaper on his way. He sat down on the bench across from the parking meter and read his paper and keep an observant eye on his surroundings. Taylor arrived at least ten minutes early. He sat and read his paper while also keeping a vigilant eye on everyone he could see as they passed him by on their route about their collective days. The usual hustle and bustle of the city he'd known all his life.

Then suddenly a vehicle pulled up abruptly, and a man dressed in a suit fit for a government agent stepped out. The man looked concerned about something as he walked from the street to the parking meter. As this was happening a woman had stopped with her stroller next to him at the end of the bench and searched through the baby's bag seemingly for something to ease the slight wine, the baby had been making. Although paying her some mind, Taylor's attention was predominantly on the man approaching the meter and rightfully so, as the man was preoccupied with Taylor as well. More so than he was supposed to be interested in the meter, seeing it was the meter he was approaching.

When the man reached the meter, he took a few moments to investigate its markings and digital screen before looking unfulfilled. The man then looked at Taylor with awkwardness before returning to his vehicle. Just then he slammed the car door shut, and sped off. The woman had still been sorting through the baby bag again as she continued to seek a satisfactory object to sooth her colloquy child. Then she leaned over to Taylor and began to speak.

"My apologies for the noise. I see that you're trying to read your paper."

Taylor smirked softly and kindly responded to the woman.

"Well to be honest I hadn't noticed that she was making much noise at all. Between the traffic and all the activity, I still can't hear her distinctly. So, I appreciate you, buy don't worry yourself. The baby is just being a baby after all."

As Taylor finished speaking, the woman looked upon him with approval. in the distance coming from the east along the sidewalk cam a new individual wearing a suit and attaché case. The usual attire for DC. The woman continued to speak to Taylor as his attention shifted to the man approaching from behind her, as she was slightly turned facing him on the bench now.

"That's kind of you to say so. You are a good man I'm sure. Only good men say things like that/ I know that your wife is a happy woman indeed. I bet she treats you like a king too. Am I right?" That last comment did throw Taylor's attention for a second. As he looked back at her and by doing so taking his eyes off of the approaching man, he became aware that he had done so just as he gazed upon her with a humorous smirk, knowing that she was potentially feeling him out to determine if he indeed was married. He wasn't certain, but felt a degree of flattery all the same. By the time he returned his glance in the direction of where the man was to have been based on his rate of travel, the man was nowhere to be seen.

Then suddenly he reappeared behind him over his left shoulder, giving him a manilla envelope as he brought Taylor to the brink of his collective cool in doing so. As fast as he discreetly handed Taylor the envelope, he walked off back into the plethora of other pedestrians and after a few seconds that man had blended back into the crowd and was gone. Before Taylor could open the envelope and investigate its contents, the woman who had been sitting next to him leaned over closer to him, attempting to show him some photos on her mobile device.

"Check out this little person. Isn't he just adorable?"

Slightly dismayed, Taylor did look at the child and reaffirmed her belief that her child was adorable. Now growing somewhat impatient to discover the contents of the envelope he had just been handed, he struggled internally to remain polite to the strange woman as she spoke to him about her child. Then she spoke again to him.

"This will help you with that also. and here is a card containing the personal mobile number for the congresswoman. on this matter use this line to communicate from here on out."

Now Taylor was definitely surprised and slightly embarrassed. She slipped him a second envelope. Then politely put her phone closer to his face, showing him an image of a baby. Then, before she collected her belongings completely, she handed him a flash drive intelligently as she reached to shake his hand before she departed.

The look on her face was not smug, more so encouraging.

With both envelopes and the flash drive stowed in the inner pocket of his jacket, Taylor found himself in a stupor of amazement. Where initially he found some amusement in being duped into falling for the mother and baby routine. That sentiment grew dark as he was increasingly uncomfortable about being so easily misled on the eve of taking on an entirely different, and more hazardous set of endeavors at the behest of his Uncle. What didn't help these epiphanies was that his danger-prone father had just popped up, and moving into a space that being so easily toyed with as he was at the park will leave him dead before long if this was how his awareness shaped up in these new endeavors. Taylor was definitely not enthused.

As he sat for just enough time for the mysterious woman and her child to fade into the pedestrian crowds before he folded his newspaper and calmly checked his watch as he stood up and walked away from the bench towards the parking lot. He took the usual detour in between points to throw off or illuminate any would be follower. Taylor took his detour and eventually found his way without a tail back to his vehicle and proceeded west on D street on his way to the coffee shop office to vet through the information he had just received.

On his way there Taylor spoke to the vehicle's Bluetooth microphone.

"Call Ox."

Shortly after providing that command, his mobile device lit up and through the car stereo system you can hear the phone ringing.

"Talk to me Spanky."

"Can you get one of the youngins to bring the silver utility van to the coffee shop and have it ready to go parked in the back for me. I am trying to save some time here and I am already a few minutes out from the office. I have some stuff to handle inside and then I will need the van to do the rest. You got me O?"

"Not a problem. I'm on it."

"Appreciate you bud. I have to meet up with my Uncle this evening for dinner, and I saw my Father earlier today, so now I know he is back in town for a minute at least. Have everyone to be even more on point. There may be a serious increase to our threat assessment. You already know why."

"Oh alright, that wassup. I knew he'd show up sooner or later with you graduating and all. But iight, do ya thang. I got you on that. the keys will be dropped directly to you. I'll send lil Mookie in to do it."

By this time Taylor had just hung a right from on D Street onto eighth. Where he took that up to E street where he made a left.

Once on E street he drove down to where it became Pennsylvania Avenue, then made a left on fourteenth. As he approached the rear of the building, he cautiously parked his vehicle and stepped out of it and hastily into the office through the backdoor. He briskly flew through the office space as he greeted his people before he found himself at the office he used most often. Taylor sat down and used the VOIP to reach out to the Congresswoman on her private line given to him through the mysterious mother.

"Hello, Chairman Willoughby? To whom may I say I am speaking to today?"

"It is Taylor Fortune."

"Taylor. I do not have this number stored for you, my apologies. I see you received my packages."

"Yes, I actually got all three. I am about to check them out and get back to you when I have something substantial to report back on. When I find something definitive."

The VOIP at that location has special security features installed that makes the line virtually impenetrable to hacking.

The associate that developed it was currently working on adapting a similar system for their mobile networks and other satellite locations.

Taylor was wrapping it up in the office just as lil Mookie ran into the office looking for him. He handed the keys off and thanked Taylor for trusting him to get it done. The two men then walked out the rear of the office and walked off in their own separate directions. Taylor then took the keys and used them to gain entry to the specially outfitted utility vehicle. He sat both of the manilla envelopes onto the counter area near one of the four workstations arranged within the sleek design of the space available. His next move was to walk into the front cabin, sit in the driver's seat and start the vehicle's ignition. Once the vehicle had been successfully started, Taylor turned on other systems housed in the console, and initiated the vehicle's security system so he could have visibility of the area outside the vehicle, and the surrounding mini parking lot.

His next move brought him swiftly back to the workstation where he sat the envelopes next to. With the monitors cycling through their respective angles of coverage overhead, Taylor continued to open the envelopes, and read carefully through their contents while he inserted the flash drive into a portal that he used to analyze the security threat of digital storage devices. Once the designated series of programs completed their process, the drive was deemed safe by the indication of a long flashing green light on the portals console. As he witnessed this development, he took the drive out from the portal and inserted it into a port on the usb hub on the countertop of the workstation.

As the mouse moved under his fingertips, navigating through folders on the drive. He looked piercingly at the main monitor nestled in between the monitors that had been displaying his outer surrounds for him. He found a folder named images of missing people. Nested under that folder were several others. What caught his eye was the folder labeled missing girls. When he double clicked that folder, an innumerable number of images populated the screen. Taylor sank back into his seat in an unfamiliar state of disbelief, as he looked into the eyes of each young woman's face on the screen, going from one image to the next.

It was at this moment that some larger picture of the world impressed upon his awareness like it had once done when he was a child, but more profound. More moving. He thought he was sitting on the top of a hill before he opened that folder with the enterprise he'd created. This changed that significantly for him. Realizing that more time had passed than he had originally noticed. He was so moved by just peeking through some of the information that he looked at his watch and decided to take the utility van to his Uncle's home directly from the coffee shop. With the hope that there was an opportunity to get his insight and assistance on the best method of approach in bringing as many of these people back to their respective loved ones.

Taylor pulled out front of the building, stepped out of the vehicle.

He was then approached by one of the building's valet attendants.

"Thank you, but I am only giving the keys to this van to Arthur tonight. Can you tell him this for me?"

The young man knowing who Taylor was, took no insult from the comment, and called Arthur on his radio.

"Lobby Door to Valet one"

Arthur responded, and came down from the office to take Taylor's Keys. Taylor told him how to secure the vehicle properly. Arthur had worked for the building since Demetrius first built it and opened its doors. So, Arthur had watched Taylor grow up, and he was familiar with his mother and Aunt. He knew he could trust

Arthur on the basis of their own relationship through the years. Artur reassured him he'd follow his instructions and keep the vehicle under observation. Taylor shook his hand, and then embraced briefly before he departed further into the building. When he arrived at his Uncle's door, as he extended his knuckles to knock on the door it opened seemingly on its own to where he had to reposition his stance so he wouldn't stumble.

Taylor, not completely surprised, began to walk into the residence. Once a place he had called his home, where he spent many of his early years after the passing of his mother. It was different for Taylor to see. Typically, when Demetrius held similar dinner parties there was much savoir fare in the atmosphere. Not this evening. The catering staff shuffled staff over the years, and some of the longer tenured members who also had seen the upbringing of that child who had just walked back through the same door as a grown man. There was definitely pride in the halls of that home at that series of moments where the staff who had watched him mature approached him with endearment and celebratory enthusiasm.

Oddly enough Taylor had apparently arrived earlier then when His Uncle had returned home from his day. Nether had his father been there. So, Taylor pulled a cigar from the humidor, clipped it and stood out on the balcony looking into the city as he lit the stogie up. He stood and blew smoke as he thought deeper on the information delivered to him hours earlier that afternoon. The faces of those young women called out to him the strongest as he attempted to figure out how to go about the business of finding any of them. One of the catering staff came out onto the balcony to check on him and he was relieved that he had done so because he had grown thirsty after smoking some of his cigar. The staff member returned shortly after they departed with a neat glass of cognac in a uniquely shaped glass that sat on the tray it was delivered on with a slant of about sixty degrees.

He reached out for the glass turning away from the balcony's edge. When he turned back towards the rail along the balcony he looked down to the street and saw a sleek black luxury sedan pull up followed by two midsize SUVs behind it. From the lead vehicle came his father and some of his uncle's security team he could readily recognize as they proceeded to attempt to stay ahead of his father's progress into the building. It was obvious to him in seeing this that his father was not entirely pleased to have the team accompany him as he went about whatever business he had to attend to while back home in the city.

Taylor thought about how his father seemed to not realize the impact he tends to have on any place he ventures through. Before long he always seems to garnish attention of negativity and increasing danger. Denard, never rattled by this, has never given Taylor the impression that he has much regard for this consistent pattern wherever he goes.

Obviously, this line of thought had roots in how the circumstances of the murders of his mother and aunt where he backlashes of his dealings and the attempt to settle some score of some kind by hurting him through the pain of hopefully hurting someone that he actually cared about. No way to know if they ever knew how deep they most likely cut him in getting to his wife. His Father was never the same after that evening, or when he finally arrived a day or so later hearing of the incident. Taylor understood why it was proper for him to go with his Uncle. He appreciated that transaction more and more at his current age.

It wasn't long before his father made his way inside the residence.

Denard had a marvelous method of charming behaviors.

and was still quite unsettling to many. He had a way of handling himself that could be awkwardly pressuring to the tinier segment of the population. To the many who also watched him, and his brother grow up within this same community that really wasn't the case. Denard was always seen home as a driven and focused man who knew what he wanted and how to go and get it. If there was a personification of by any means necessary, it would have to be his father. Moments later Denard also stepped out onto the balcony with his own cigar and drink in hand.

Neither men overrun with the desire to participate in extended emotional displays, private or public, shared the balcony with some space between where they both stood. As the two men stood silently by the railing, blowing smoke into the air and occasionally pouring their alcoholic beverages into their mouths. They just stood there initially observing their view of the city. The silence was then broken when Denard chose to inhale and release a long stream of thick smoke in some loose shape.

"I am proud of you."

Taylor turned slightly, eyebrows raising slightly.

Denard continued to speak.

"According to your uncle, you've completed your master's degree, started a business with a unique cache of niche services, and established a well-organized team of longtime associates to manage this with you. I am not surprised by Taylor. You're a remarkable young man. I am grateful that after all that has happened you did not let any of it prevent you from making a way for yourself"

Both men took a brief pause as Taylor's eye brows were still slightly elevated, watching his father's facial expression as he spoke.

"Now you want to take a new path, huh? Do you see yourself as being ready to take on this new challenge? It may be similar in the root to much of what you deal with every day in what you've created, but the situations surrounding everything after you start will drastically change and can never be reversed once the change begins."

Now at that last remark Taylor took another drink from his snifter, as he then placed it on the rail. He drew in another pull on his cigar as he looked into his father's eyes with a blank expression across his face as all that could be derived from his demeanor was that he was preparing his mouth to speak.

"Well... yes, Pops. I have decided to follow up on seeing what Uncle D was referring to in regards to the work the two of you share occasionally. I see no reason to be discouraged by any fear of the unknown I may develop. Right now, I have no such fear. But from watching what you have going on with and around you I know I will see just what you've said become real for me in some ways before long. I hope to be ready for that when it does happen. The slight anxiety of how and when that happens is keeping me on my mental toes actually."

Intrigued by the manner and choice of words that comprised his son's response, Denard continued to stand by the railings corner as he gave the body language signals that he was going to just listen to what his son had to say before he was going to speak again. So, Taylor, seeing this continued to speak.

"I wasn't officially motivated to take this route initially, but things have changed, and shockingly so has my perspective of what doing this can mean to me, and what I am already doing. I'm definitely not you. Not saying that with any negativity, just acknowledging that we think differently and take differing directional paths in how we make decisions. If this will work for me, I need to customize my involvement. I don't need to do the things that are better suited for you and your skill sets Pops... maybe that can be a possibility in time. Not now however. Now I need to find my own lane and grow there. I do think that at some point in time our differences may actually serve to complement one another. As far as risks go, the enlargement of my business dealings here alone would eventually create risks of their own. I cannot let real risk or potential risk curve my decisions ever. I will use them to build a set of contingencies around but not ever will I allow it to shun me away from an objective."

Taylor paused again to gauge whether or not he would see the same response from his father as he had just before. Denard's expression slightly morphed into a slightly proud and inquisitive smirk that almost seemed like he was proud to hear his son speak like he had been.

"I see now that I have more to learn than I had initially thought. I won't let that learning process intimidate my desire to find my niche in this. get to my strong suits and identify my areas in need of improvement. Even if I have to face the fact that I may not have any of the abilities at the moment to make this work out the gate. I will adapt and I will improve myself in this process."

Denard, still with the smirking expression put his snifter now to his mouth, took a long sip, and as he swirled the contents of the beverage around in his mouth looked around at their view of the city. He then turned directly facing his son and began to respond.

"You've said a lot. I understand where you're coming from, or so I think that I do. I respect your approach, and I want you to know that albeit that this endeavor is no comical matter, but it also exacts from you eventually one hell of a toll before it may just snuff you out. This goes for me yet. I try my best to stay three moves ahead of the toll collector every moment of just about every one of each day I have at this point. We fight the fight that is not overly approved to have anyone fighting for. Know this above most of what you may learn. This lies at the core of all of this. If that turns out to not be the case be mindful of your surroundings and who is directing who."

Taylor now was intrigued for several reasons after hearing father speak on the subject. Taylor took in additional totes on his cigar as his father continued to speak with him.

"This is the business of handling matters that concern matters of extreme importance to the threads of this democracy. Many are out here right now doing the same thing under the motivations and influences of different men, with different visions for what the future of this nation ought to embody, ought to look like. This makes the landscape challenging. Even I have conducted some activities that many would consider devout of morality. I see that clearer today in hindsight more so than did I when the decision had been made to have me facilitate decisions made by other individuals."

"And that's real Son! So, use that brilliance of yours to understand this and do better than I did when I started. I hadn't anticipated the connection to such thinking in relation to what I initially thought this was. Neither did my brother exactly. But what did we lose as a result of me not knowing how to do this? More than I care to acknowledge at the moment, more than I could ever imagine on how to begin to even partially repair. That is a debilitating realization Son."

Taylor simply nodded his head in admiration of the honesty his father shared with him. He was at this point even more driven to proceed. He'd already lost more than he could lose again. There was never left to lose for him in this. Nothing to lose but who he was. He thought about that as he continued to drink his beverage. His father succeeded. His words sank deep within him. Had Taylor thinking for a moment about how to effectively focus and commit his mind to seeing this through and formulating the best set of contingencies for his team and remaining family members close enough to him that could possibly become vulnerable due to these pending decisions he intended to definitely act upon.

With that conversation behind them, Taylor turned back towards the railing facing the city and resumed his gaze out onto the bustling atmosphere of the city as the evening grew darker from the sun disappearing even further beyond sight into the horizon. Denard recognized that his son not disrespectfully turned his back on him, yet rather he was further contemplating the content of what he shared with him in addition to what he could only guess as the countless other things that could have been on his son's mind. He hadn't seen Taylor in about two years. Things move fast in DC, and he knew this reality translated into feeling more like missing five years of his son's life.

He knew he was not in town for very long, and he also knew that he did not have the time available to him for there to be any real effective amount of quality time with his son. As both of them were now back to their original positions, gazing out onto the city's commencement of evening activities.

After about five minutes of silence, a small motorcade approached the building. In the middle of two SUVs drove Demetrius's vehicle of choice. Instinctively, a member of his catering staff ran out onto the balcony where Taylor and Denard had been standing, peeked over the rail, and then jogged back into the residence loudly enough informing the other members of their team that Delegate Fortune had arrived. Their pace quickened collectively, and the finalization of their preparation for the evening's events became visibly closer to coming together rather quickly. Demetrius was continuously followed by a small swarm of his staff at most points of his day except for that entourage following him past his front door. It was his long-standing decree that if they come beyond the threshold of his residence, they are off the clock, and barring a national emergency, so is he at that point.

His staff indeed followed him to the threshold and then returned to the elevator as they busily began their jump on the dealings pertaining to their attempts at being a step ahead of tomorrow. What the Delegate would expect of them all. Demetrius's personal staff approached him and assisted him in taking off his overcoat and jacket. He briefly, but affectionately searched the residence for his brother and nephew as he continued to make his way through the residence on his way to his bathroom to shower and prepare for dinner with his family. He saw a glimpse of them on the balcony; he smiled briefly knowing that they were speaking and moved briskly into his bedroom that led to his bathroom.

Demetrius, after attending to his personal hygiene needs strolled from beyond the grand doors into his bedroom out into the open living space. He ventured out onto the balcony where he found his brother and nephew just standing by the rail with a respectable distance between one another as they smoked and drank. Both of their cigars had almost reached the limit of their smokable usage. This didn't stop Demetrius from grabbing his own cigar from his assistant, who had also brought him his drink the way he preferred it as well. Demetrius stood in between the two with coincidentally enough space to wrap his arms around each of them without straining.

"This is a glorious occasion indeed. We haven't had many opportunities to do what we are doing right now in our lifetimes. Now with Taylor being a grown man himself, this is a monumental evening without question!"

The two of them remained silent as Demetrius continued to speak.

"I have some excellent food for us to enjoy tonight. I have a guest that will join us around the time of desert, so be aware of that. Just the one. It may become a night that takes us into the morning, I am not entirely sure. Regardless, I am openly and officially sharing the fact that I am very much so a happy man because I have my family here with me under this one roof. Not a normal or frequent occurrence. Enough to celebrate all to itself."

To this Tylor considered that he alone was aware of subjects he planned on discussing with the two of them. Pending the announcement of the arrival of the guest to come, there was quite a bit he had wanted to obtain from them both. He had taken some initiative on this work with Chairman Willoughby, whom he had already assumed with certainty was just a front for his uncle. So, once they got past the irony of that and the humor attached to it depending on the perspective of his father, uncle, or himself. Either way, he just felt like when he saw his opportunity to get to the heart of the matter that he had to pounce on it despite any discomfort it may produce. This amidst seeing the apparent jubilance of the reunion energy in the sentiment of his Uncle's opening words.

Demetrius continued to speak to them, and communicate concerns to his catering staff as they were just about at the end of their preparation duties, with the table not completely set. With the entire home teeming with wondrous aromas that would severe the adherence to any hunger strike known to man.

"Yeah buddy! I skipped on finishing some of my lunch to leave room for this meal. We will be busy I'm sure so let's eat now."

Demetrius walked off the balcony, and into the mix of caterers speeding through his kitchen and dining room, as he assisted in the direction of having the table ready with food for their meal. As Demetrius tightened the screws on their techniques with his style of motivational encouragement, Taylor and his Father followed him from a distance into the dining room. Taylor walked behind his father as he thought of what his Uncle actually had said to them. He was uncertain who his uncle would bring to such a dinner that would interfere with the whole reunion vibe he'd been kicking around all day once the presence of his father was all the way out the bag. Worst case scenario he thought had been that his desired first task was being brought with them? Hopefully if that was the case that the guest was the Congresswoman he'd communicated earlier, since he had already suspected that she was just a face for his uncle to begin with. Unsure of which would be the case, or the equally intriguing possibility that it was nether.

So, with his mind working, the two of them approach the dining room table taking their seats. Denard sat at the opposite end from where Demetrius was set up to have sat at if he wasn't micromanaging the kitchen team slightly. Taylor chose a seat on the lengthy side of the table facing the entrance to the home. Eventually Demetrius, once more comfortable in the arrival of the meal from out of the kitchen to the table, took his seat and they began to have their plates prepared and passed around. Before they dug into their plates one of the caterers blessed the food, and they started to eat. The food was obviously delicious because not a word had been spoken for at least twenty minutes from when they started to eat. Then finally, Demetrius pulled back from the table with a sigh and a pleased look upon his face.

"That was great! Wow! I ate quite a bit tonight. I will need to get two hours into this workout tonight somehow, we'll see how that works."

Denard and Taylor both were coming close to finishing off their respective plates as well.

"So, Taylor. I just want to tell you that I am proud of how far you've come considering the time and some of the potential distractions that would have easily distracted many others from being able to utilize the focus that you have and how you have already accomplished so much for such a young man with immense promise."

"I agree. I know my version of Fatherhood is not normal nor does it allow me to be present for all your moments. My Brother, you Uncle is here with me through it all so I can continue to uphold a promise I've made long before You began to breathe the life given to you. I could not be any prouder of you as I am right now being the young man you are today. This can only intensify."

Taylor, knowing that his moment had just presented itself on a platter no less, stood up with his wine glass in one hand, and the other holding a bottle of sweet red they often drank, and poured more into his cup. He then continued to pour more into his father's and uncle's cups before he spoke to them both.

"I can appreciate being celebrated by two accomplished individuals such as the two of you kingpins in your respective fields. I had a period of time early on where I had not much focus at all. I wasn't sure what I thought about life at that moment. Let alone my place in it. But due to the wisdom given to me from you both, and your sponsorship Uncle D through the rough years here in the halls of this home made a huge impact. At this very table I formulated several plans that eventually laid seed to what me and the guys have running today."

This pleased both men as they eagerly listened to what he was saying to them. Taylor continued, working at accomplishing his goal of bridging the whole array of subjects.

"With that, I want to raise this cup and give all of us this praise. My success is something to celebrate in some part, but if not for the involvement of the two of you and others, I would not have come this far. That's real and sincere from my heart."

Taylor raised his glass even slightly higher by just a hair as he then brought the flute to his lips and began to drink his beverage. Once all three of them did the same, there was a moment of silence that comprised each of them sharing non-verbal eye contact and unspoken acceptance to the words previously spoken.

A second swig from their beverages was then activated. After this Taylor who was still standing, spoke once more.

"We are Fortune's. We deal with the heart of all matters, and we do so with diligence, resilience, and relentless devotion. I am about to follow both of you in a direction that will change my life as I know it will be forever more. In acceptance of this, I entertained work recently that I normally would not have. In doing so, I immediately have seen how small the world I am leaving is in comparison to the one in which I am entering into. I know I need the assistance and active involvement from the both of you to get me started properly and more than likely continuously over time as what I do will in doubt involve the two of you in varying degrees of complexity. With all that said I have some information in a secured mobile workstation downstairs we must walk through before we call this evening officially over, in regards to business."

Taylor took his flute and drank from it once more, finishing its contents before he somewhat roughly returned it to the table. Just shortly after that moment, a chime rang from the foyer signaling that there were guests at the front door.

"Our guests have arrived I see." Demetrius responded.

Taylor looked slightly deflated as their arrival came on the cusp of his statement that he had hoped would evoke some response that he could use to build their enthusiasm in taking this gathering to the vehicle or even better into his Uncle's conference room down the hall. None of this had any time to take place however. Demetrius stood up as one of his catering staff approached him to announce the identification of his guests. This news came as no surprise to him as he gestured for them to be led into the dining hall.

"Gentlemen, allow me to first introduce my colleague from DC, Chairman of the council Mrs. Vanessa Willoughby. And with her we have one of our fine constituents, Mrs. Yolanda Rhodeson from East Washington Heights. What do I have the honor of hosting you in my home tonight ladies? Please have a seat and we will bring you both out a plate and fill your glasses."

As his catering staff accommodated his newly arrived guests and got them both situated and comfortable. Demetrius took the opportunity to depart the room and move quickly around his home as if anticipating the group moving into another room. Although the timing of the doorbell interrupted his nephew's momentum, he had not been distracted from what he had said. He was informed by Arthur about the utility van and recognized that there must have been something he wanted to share. So, he took a moment to have his home assistant to have his conference room prepared for the eventual migration into that space. He anticipated this to be the outcome of their visit, let alone the next step in following up with where Taylor was leading them.

Meanwhile Taylor and Denard were in the dining hall exchanging moderate pleasantries with Chairman Willoughby and Mrs. Rhodeson. Chairman Willoughby, consistent with her reputation for being a straight shooter, began to address both of the men before her.

"Well Taylor, you are the one I came out this evening to speak to. We already began this conversation. I brought Mrs. Rhodeson to give it some depth. GO on Ma'am tell him what you need him to know... help him understand you."

It was visibly seen that Mrs. Rhodeson was uneasy having been put in such a spot. She took a moment to collect herself and get her thoughts arranged with the hopes of not embarrassing herself on the spot too much as she started to softly speak.

"Well... To get right to it both my niece Zenobia, and her young daughter Zoey have been missing for about a week. My niece knows that I get worried over her, and since I take care of Zoey for her a few times a week while her niece worked it had her extremely concerned when I failed to hear from her for over five days. Mrs. Chairman Willoughby here has given me her word that she has a very talented group of professionals looking into it. We all know about you Denard, and some of us have even heard of you Taylor. We all know that Delegate Fortune will not settle for any defeat of any kind, so I am at ease knowing that you all are the professionals she had referred to."

Both Denard and Taylor readjusted themselves in their seats as she spoke to them. Both men were sincerely attentive to her every word. Seeing that she had their full attention she grew more comfortable in speaking as she continued.

"At first I had my suspicions concerning the guy I knew of that she had been seeing off and on again. He was a very jealous, shady fellow. I never particularly cared for him because of not only how I witnessed him speaking to my niece when he didn't think anyone was paying attention, but what my ladies in the neighborhood said that they knew of him as well. Some of them watched him grow up and knew he was trouble for my niece. Just bad news all around. I had encouraged her to let that man go many times, but I do not believe she actually took my advice."

At that moment Demetrius had made his way back into the dining hall. He had one of his caterers assist the ladies and their drinks into the conference room down the hall.

"C'mon ladies, and gentlemen. I will have your plates brought into the conference room shortly. We can make better use of the time and get to the bottom of all of this, or as close as any meeting will get us. We still have to go out and handle our business. Which we certainly will."

As the group populates into the lavish room filled with all varieties of technological delight, Demetrius had one of his assistants prepare the screen to display the information from the workstation. The first image that was displayed on the screen was apparently a live video feed from the parking garage. The screen showed Arthur standing near Taylor's utility van. This intrigued Taylor obviously. Then suddenly a much wider and larger utility van pulled in front of the previously displayed van eclipsing it completely.

"Really? Uncle Demetrius!"

Lamented Taylor. Shifting in his chair with a dampening to his demeanor. Demetrius carried on as Arthur walked into the larger utility vehicle and set up the comm link to the conference room. Next, Demetrius pulled up images of both Zenobi and Zoey, along with an additional screen showcasing their background information and last known addresses. On a different screen He Brought up an image of the man Mrs. Rhodeson had mentioned earlier as a person of interest in the disappearance.

"Here we have the young mother and daughter shown here. alongside them we have the gentlemen that Mrs. Rhodeson believes may have some involvement in her niece's disappearance. His name happens to be Ronald Evans. Him we know because he actually works for Manny, who works for Pasqualle, who works with Khaleel. So, finding him and getting information from him should not be difficult. Without knowing much beyond this here what we want from Ronald is a last public location where he was with her. With that I can gain access to the city's closed-circuit camera feed with the authorization of Chairman Willoughby. We will then be able to track her through the system until she specifically went off the grid. and where she went off the grid will be where we begin this investigation."

To this Taylor stood and pulled a device out of his pocket around the size of a flash drive and gestured to his Uncle for permission to insert it into his workstation. His Uncle agreed, and gave him the nod to do so. Taylor then plugged the device into the workstation, manned its keyboard and began to insert a series of commands into the computer. Soon after, on the last screen available on the wall popped up a feed to his utility van showcasing the information he was referring to earlier before the women had arrived.

"What I have here, courtesy of Chairman Willoughby is information that we may also want to have dear old Ronnie to chime in on. When we do run into him. There are apparently several young women and children missing in the city recently, over the past two months alone. Now where these women are also of grave concern for us all for all the obvious reasons. First and most important of all that these are our women from our community. I know that none of us are going to stand for this in our community so We need to figure out where they are taking these women and children. Then we can find out who has them, and to eventually shed light on who has been involved with taking them from this neighborhood. So, we can handle our business, our way."

And again, he set his screen to automatic slow scroll as it displayed countless women who had been declared missing and the information related to their disappearances.

"I believe there exists an excellent opportunity in the midst of how things have developed, despite how disturbing it has been. We already have leads into finding when Zenobia and her daughter fell off the grid. We will definitely be able to use the information we currently have to our overall benefit. This has already given us a chance to find out how the abduction took place."

Taylor paused as he spoke and gazed around the conference room into the eyes of the other people to enhance the emphasis of his words to them. Then he continued to speak.

"Uncle Demetrius, when you get that footage, and find in it what I will need to search down the next set of information, you know how to relay that to me. in the meantime, I will find out when these other women fell out of touch as well, so I can have you do the same on their behalf. We need to bring them all home as fast as possible."

Ever the more motivated, Taylor stood up from the table, pulled a mobile device from his inner pocket, dialed in a number and started to speak into the device as he gestured his good evenings to the occupants of the dining hall as he departed the residence. Both Demetrius and Denard were equally impressed by the demonstration of initiative by Taylor as he hurried back on the trail, he was starting to take in finding his way through the information provided. While Demetrius knew that his hospitality for Mrs. Rhodeson and Councilwoman Willoughby would require the reminder of his evenings time. Denard, who was eager to join his son, had needed to find the appropriate cause to get out of the building. Then Demetrius took the opportunity within the silence after Taylor had just left to speak,

"Ladies... Allow my brother to leave us be as he has his own list of information to track down and verify. Denard, Take the dark brow folder and catch up to Tylor so the two of you can be more productive. Show him what it means to have come into the Unit."

Denard, grateful for the properly laid exit left the dining room as he raced out the home to find his son.

CHAPTER 8

"Honed in"

As Demetrius had remained as the good host to Council Woman Willoughby, and Mrs. Rhodeson, The three of them continued on to have their meal for dinner. In doing so, they each carried on with a sense of heightened accomplishment in their collective confidence regarding Denard and Taylor's endeavors on behalf of Mrs. Rhodes and the other parents in similar circumstances. Denard finally caught up with Taylor in the parking garage working in his Utility Van. Going back and forth between the one he came in, and his Uncle's larger one parked alongside of it. Arthur stood on the side as he continued to manage and coordinate the movements of his valet team.

"What's going down Mr. Arthur? You still looking really young out here"

Arthur nodded, and responded with a slight grin as the lighting overhead shone off his gold tooth.

"I see you still looking like you got that quick footwork. I peeped you pop up out of nowhere just like you did before you left town the first time. You always were a quick one."

Demetrius nodded back with reverence, and spoke again.

"True indeed. Things are heating up, Mr. Arthur. We will be needing to have you sit down with the Pounders very soon.

Taylor will be coming with us. We are getting him started now. I will send word when the time has come."

Taylor was on his mobile device again when Denard had made his way to the threshold of the door to peek into the cabin to see what his Son had been working on.

"Hey pops. I'm on the phone. Can you go to Uncle D's Van and get on the active workstation there as I finish following this thread I am on now? I have three lined out from the list of the names on his network. Once we get all of this done I will reach out to the team, and we will follow up on as many of these people that we can hopefully all at the same time in case of the result of us making contact in pursuing the disappearance of any one particular person would set off any contingencies these guys may have established for the potential of avoiding any intrusive investigation such as ours from being able to penetrate their tracks and find anything that we can take to get deeper insight into any identities or organizational structure that they have been operating under."

Denard, even more impressed with the tenacity in his son's devotion to getting closer to a breakthrough out the gate. So, he took the direction and left that van and proceeded to go into the cabin of the van belonging to his younger brother. Once there, he pulled up the communications system and sent Taylor a video conference link for the two to communicate and see one another as they did so. Taylor did not have the exact tools to facilitate such a call in his van but all that he had been lacking was the software. Once he communicated that to his father, Denard just assembled that specific program and a slew of other useful ones together and sent him the software care package. Once Taylor opened it on the other end the software installed itself immediately. It was a lot more of a care package than he initially had in mind. The process of taking on the upgrade did force him to reboot the system for about three minutes however. This wasn't what Taylor had in mind. When the system came back online, he was no longer frustrated. The group of programs completely revamped his system altogether. Denard now appearing in a window along the top of one of his several monitors leaned into the camera saying,

"Your part of this team now. Our Unit is a small part of a larger, more focused team. Even just being fresh to the Unit, you have access to state-of-the-art everything now. We have teams of scholars performing research and development, on other teams of engineers performing their own research and developments on cutting edge technologies that we deem to be useful in the field. So, we have most of what you want and need. I also envision you as the one who will keep them quite busy with the suggestions and ideas from that brain of yours."

Taylor was still trying not to get overly distracted, as he teamed with awe peeking through the myriad of hierarchical upgrades to his systems. He caught himself, and snapped out of his preoccupied state of curiosity, and spoke back to his Father through the screen.

"Ok Pops. What I need is for you to take that energy and upgrade my office network systems. Can you do that for me as well? No point in me utilizing substandard equipment on any level or my team. They extend my efficacy as you will soon discover. Thank you for the upgrade though. Can I get some documentation on the ins and outs as well so I can train my staff on the inner workings of this deployment?"

Through the screen Taylor could see Denard going through his mobile device and seem like he found what he was looking for as he pressed his finger to its screen, then simply said back to his

Son,

"DONE. Do you trust me Taylor?", asked Denard.

"Yes. I do.", Replied Taylor.

"Then open this link I am about to send to you. Once you do, it will utilize your phone's security protocols to access your network server that you normally communicate through to your system and it will then deploy a package we had designed specifically for you to enhance systems you may have in operation already, or significantly enhance everything you have overall. Within it will be several training manuals that will be encrypted, and only accessible by biometric security measures. Your Uncle was waiting on me to give him the signal that signified that we had this discussion so he can have some new peripheral upgrades couriered over to your Coffee Shop. In that series of deliveries will be the biometric equipment to facilitate the newly upgraded systems. If you go through all that and still find gaps in efficiency just let me or your Uncle know. Then we will work on having that deficiency rectified as immediately as feasibly possible."

"That sounds fantastic.", Responded Taylor.

"OK. Pops, what are you running over there since you obviously have all the technological insight tonight? Do you have something that will do our computer work for us both and vet this information for results to connect any of these dots for us out here?", Taylor continued.

Denard responded initially by tapping his finger on the camera lens. Then he said,

"As a matter of fact, I do. If you look carefully on your screen, I can navigate you to where you now have it as well. check your chat I sent a text file showing the hierarchical tree to the program you will need to run."

As the speakers on Taylor's end chimed, indicating that his computer had just received a chat message. Within the message there was an attachment. Taylor swiftly moved his hand along the top of his mouse as it maneuvered its corresponding icon on the screen to over where the attachment symbol was located on the screen. As Taylor clicked it, the attachment downloaded and the text file populated onto the screen. Taylor then spoke to his father,

"Ok, I have the text file opened. It seems pretty straight forward enough."

As Taylor was speaking to his father, he was following the instructions from the on-screen text file. Once he arrived at the fil destination, he simply double clicked on the icon for the new program and it opened up a three-dimensional image on the screen in high definition of a classic hotel concierge. Across the concierge's stomach section was an empty text box. Next to the interior end of the text box's right edge was a symbol of a microphone.

"What do you see Taylor? Tell me what came across your screen after you double clicked the program icon?", Asked Denard.

Taylor responded,

"I see the hotel concierge figure, the text box with the microphone image in its right corner?"

"Good, that's what I was hoping to hear that you were looking at.

Actually, click on this link too.", Said Denard.

"You're going to remote link it?", Taylor asked quickly.

"Yup. Standby."

Now once their workstations became linked Denard walked Taylor through the process of either typing the query into the text box and initiating a program to find a solution, as well as how to operate the request through the microphone option illustrated by the mic image in the text box corner. Denard walked Taylor through the process of asking the program to search through countless documents and utilizing the litany of algorithmic protocols designed to analyze the data in a dynamic fashion, flexibly based to interpret the selected information through the specific query parameters.

"The developers referred to the Gadget as 'Cosmo', yet it was officially entitled 'Cosmic'."

"So, once your system undergoes the forty-eight-hour system security evaluation protocol, a next transmission will be initiated. This recommended security standard will be installed throughout your server and connected systems. You and your team should know to expect daily security scans from our main signal server. These scans will conduct themselves in the background and will not interfere with the operations of your interoffice activities. With that, let me bounce back to 'Cosmo'. 'Cosmo' is our personal artificial intelligence service program. He was designed to resolve any and all potential queries you may have to submit. So, if you were to ask 'Cosmo', 'Hey Cosmo, Take the documents I am placing on your desk, and cross reference their contents in their entirety for any connections along these described categories:

[Pause], related areas of disappearance. [Pause], Related ages. [Pause], Related historical residence histories. [Pause], then cross reference any similarities from each of the individuals listed in the file to include any shared known associates of any kind. Thank you, Cosmo."

Taylor was quite attentive as his father was breaking down the AI interface to him. His mind was virtually bursting at it seems in anticipation of seeing how he could possibly take this option to its conceivable precipice.

"So, to close out the query in oration I'd tell 'Cosmo', 'Thank you'.", Taylor asked.

"Exactly!", Responded Denard.

Now Denard, seeing that his son was absorbing the information continued to speak across the monitor,

"Now, I will move this master folder on your desktop over to the folder icon near 'Cosmo's hand which is his 'desk'. Once this is done I can either press 'F7' or say 'initiate Cosmo', and the AI will begin the process that you instructed it to undergo."

Taylor leaned back into his chair and seemed to show an appreciation for how the process worked. As he was in that position, Denard continued once more,

"Now, we just allow the system to render its computations and evaluation of the information submitted and ultimately an outcome. Since what we need to move forward is essentially what we are waiting on the system to best identify for us from the stacks of data, we can just work on other related aspects of the investigations and map out what we will do potentially with the results. So, plan the next move in the meantime."

"Well what Cosmo should provide, if I had to imagine... would be a list of the victims who have similarities in the matters related to their disappearances. Within that, there may be some information that can take us closer to the circumstances involved in their abductions. If this turns out to be the case, we can then tap into the municipal cctv feeds Uncle D mentioned to playback the events of the incidents with the hopes of finding visual evidence that will lead us to additional names of individuals we can run through Cosmo for evaluation. As we go through all the people that can be physically connected to the abductions, we run them all through Cosmo and we will eventually filter through the group to find who we need to start having my people seek out with the hopes of surveilling them and lead us to their associates and or the missing people."

Denard now sat back into his chair. there was a moment of silence as Denard sat there with an expression across his face positive realization. Then he stood up from his chair and walked off screen. Suddenly he appeared at the threshold of Taylor's van and spoke.

"I completely agree. Now what did you have in mind?"

Taylor now stricken with an epiphany, used his fingers to gesture to his father to give him a minute. Then as he did so he pulled a mobile device out of his pocket, and then he dialed into it a series of numbers. As the phone started to ring its recipient Taylor sat patiently awaiting the call to be answered. Langston answered. "Yoo."

"Hey Cuz, was you serious the other night when you said that you were gonna take this ride with me and Uncle D?"

"You know I was T."

"Ok. Then that time has come. I need you to come to me at Uncle D's spot. The loft. Get to Mr. Arthur, and he'll take you to where I am in the parking garage."

"Bet that up T. On my way." Taylor turned to Denard.

"Langston needs to be a part of this process as well. That man wants to get involved, and see where this goes just as I do. He's got more at stake in getting down with this move than even I do. I lost my Mother and any chance of living the life she wanted for me, and he lost the same in addition to damn near everything else that ever mattered to him. Possibly whatever could have mattered to him. So, when Cosmo is complete, we will have more than enough to do. We will need quite a few competent people on this. In addition to what Langston will without question bring to the table."

As the two of them sat across from one another inside the larger utility van, and allowed for the tone and content of Taylor's words to sink deeper into the atmosphere. When suddenly there sounded off a distinct chime from the workstation. Cosmo had produced its report. Denard seemed reassured, whereas Taylor, still learning about Cosmo's performance capabilities, was now interested to see the effectiveness in its findings for himself. Both of them rolled and scooted their chairs towards the screen that displayed the read-out. It read out to them a short dossier for each of the missing women. Within that certain data sets were highlighted. pertinent case related information such as the time of day each woman had been reportedly abducted or pronounced missing, the day of the week the event allegedly took place, the height and weight of each woman, the last documented location each woman had been seen at before their disappearance, and any names of those suspected in their disappearances.

from the twenty dossier files submitted into the system with additional documentation pertaining to all the missing person reports the system kicked back a list of five names; Claudine

Miller, Alissa Rodriguez, Noreen Martin, Benita Garcia, and Paige Jackson. Coincidently there was a name mentioned in the preliminary report furnished by Cosmo that brought Ronald Evans name back into question. He was linked to one of the missing women as a recent romantic interest. The woman's name he was associated with was Noreen Martin.

She was affiliated with another of the five women in Cosmo's report. Alissa Rodriguez. Alissa was a romantic interest of a known associate of Evans, an Efren Hernandez.

As it turned out, there was an additional woman associated with

Hernandez. Her name was Melita Delgado. Both Efren and Ronald worked at the Brandmaxx distribution warehouse out near Alexandria, Virginia. There was a third man named in the report to have had romantic association with the two remaining women on the list of women with connecting threads. His name was Theodore Wright. There wasn't much information on Wright in the preliminary report. So Denard set Cosmo to dig further into the background of Wright as Taylor and him discussed the necessity of paying a visit to the distribution warehouse across the river in Virginia. What was also mentioned initially within the preliminary reports was how there had been multiple reports of domestic violence as indicated through several police reports, but no mention of any active or previously filed orders of protection or any restraining orders.

Unsure as to what these similarities and connective details meant overall, Denard and Taylor were left to decide what their next move was going to be.

"We know where to find Ronald, and we were looking for him anyway. Now we have more than a few reasons to speak with him. I'm thinking that Demetrius can give us the drop and avoid any suspicion until we have Ronald and hopefully Efren too, where we need them blocked off. I don't feel like chasing anyone."

When Denard finished speaking, Taylor briefly responded.

"Yeah, I'd prefer to avoid that. There will be two of them. That facility is rather large. We'd definitely be in a better position if we could box them in and avoid being separated."

Denard agreed with his son. Again, the both of them took a moment of silence to further evaluate plans of approach and additional contingencies. Shortly after they began to do this Langston was approaching the area of the street that led to the cul de sac where the residence was positioned. Unbeknownst to him, he had been followed by a similar looking vehicle to another vehicle seen following Tayler on previous occasions. Langston made short work of the distance between himself and the Utility vans on the private section of the parking deck. The vehicle that had been tailing him from a distance had stopped following him once they came to the beginning of the street where he turned down towards Demetrius's building. Just as Langston was pulling around into the parking complex adjacent to the building, a second vehicle pulled up alongside the sedan that had been tailing Langston. It was a black on black heavily tinted windowed SUV. A window on each vehicle had rolled down slowly and the men began to speak across vehicles. Their conversation was brief. The SUV pulled off after only having stopped for about a minute at best. After the vehicle that was originally following Langston had also pulled off just as a third vehicle, a sedan of different make pulled up from the opposite side of the street and parked with its smokey tinted windows rolled all the way up.

Langston parked alongside the Valet section and briefly spoke to Arthur. Arthur then gave him the access to where the vans had been parked. By the time he pulled up on Taylor and Denard, they had just exited the larger of the two utility vans.

"Ok I am here. Now what?", Langston had asked.

"Well, my Father is about to get some things arranged with Uncle D upstairs, then we will be heading out to Virginia to follow a lead on a case we just received. Some human trafficking related issues. I want you to get tooled up and come with us. We need you to establish a perimeter and monitor it while we are there in case, we find ourselves in a chase situation.", Responded Taylor.

"Now that's what I want to hear! Ok, I am going to get some equipment from an office close by.", Langston grew visibly excited.

"That won't be necessary Spike, Open the rear wall panel in our van. You should be good with what's in there."

As Langston followed Taylor's instructions to the rear of the Utility van he drove there, Taylor re-entered the larger van and went back to reading the details of the information produced by Cosmo. Shortly after he did so Langston entered the van behind him quite exuberant in what he had found in the smaller van. At this time Langston's' raw enjoyment of the new found equipment abruptly ended as he took notice of all the information sprawled out across the multi-screen display system of the workstation. All the faces, and their background information took him by surprise instantly once his attention shifted to see them.

"What the hell is all this T?", Langston exclaimed.

Taylor was somewhat distracted in his readings to respond to

Colin at that moment. Langston now pacing through the workspace inside the van taking notice of the same information that Taylor was preoccupied in. The two of them remained silent as they both familiarized themselves with reading the data displayed across the myriad of screens.

At this time Denard had returned. He acknowledged Langston's arrival.

"Hey Nephew! You're getting brolic on us all! Man, it's really good to see you, and even better knowing you making this move with the family Langston. I am her for anything you need in any capacity. Neither one of you will be alone in this at any time. Well not for long or without a relentless effort to rectify the situation for your benefit."

Both of the young men stood silent and attentive to his words and the sentiment he exuded with them.

"Now as for the next move, here it is...", Denard continued to speak.

"Me and Taylor will use the credentials and conduct a random inspection on the Distribution warehouse as OSHA Officials. Langston you monitor the perimeter as best you can place a focus on maintaining communication with us in case, we have runners. We will be seeking to gather the two men and bring them to a secure office in the distribution center."

Denard then input some data into Cosmo and on a screen amongst the rest as it replaced what was previously displayed on it with a schematic layout of the warehouse. With this Denard explained what room he intended to bring the two persons of interest into, and the pathway in which they would go about this plan.

"At this point we can assume no one is aware of our intentions, so once we make contact that will no longer be the case and everything from that point will have changed. They will have the drop on us. We must keep this in mind because they will know who we are, and we will not know who any of them are. There is no need to explain the detriment in that. But, that's how the game is played when you're investigating things that others will not appreciate you investigating. This is the job. Revenge and bitterness are also a bi-product of the business."

"So, Langston Go to Arthur and have him bring me the recognizance vehicle. He will know what you're referring to.", Denard said to Langston.

"Taylor, I will be going through the materials here until he gets back, which should not be long. You are free to join me or whatever other preparations you need to attend to. Once he returns, we will be heading out."

The both of them parsed through the information produced through Cosmos. As they continued to examine their plan of action.

"What we need to do is first secure both Ronald and Efren. Once we have them both secured, we can then work them both for any pertinent information on the whereabouts of this Mr. Wright character, and more importantly, how these men are connected to the disappearances of these five women. With any glimpse of a break, we can find information that will lead us to finding all of these women."

Taylor listened sternly as his father spoke to him. He agreed with his father's perspective on the situation. Shortly after Denard spoke and Taylor took some moments to further consider what was said, then not long after that Langston arrived back with the customized SUV. Within the cockpit of the vehicle Langston was finishing up a telephone conversation with his older brother, advising him of his eventually required involvement in the search for these women from the neighborhood. Before Langston was able to completely exit the vehicle, or end his conversation with Vaughn, Denard and Taylor had already converged on the vehicle, opened the rear gate, packed an assortment of bags into it before doubling back to the front of the vehicle where they jumped in. Langston frustratedly hopped the half of his body that made it out of the truck back into it. Next, since everyone involved had been in the cockpit, Langston then transferred the call to the sound system in the truck. Now Vaughn was a part of the conversation, Langston set forth the introduction.

"Ok Bro, you're live!"

There was some initial static disruption before Vaughn started to speak.

"I know that I need to tool the hell up knowing that the two of you are in the same place at the same time. God dammit! Uncle Deny you have a horrible track record with your visits and the safety of those connected to you. No doubt this whole city is about to get a taste of what you got in store. No doubt."

Taylor leaned over and was about to respond to Vaughn until Denard's hand had tapped him on his shoulder forcibly enough to indicate that he was going to respond first...

"Vaughn... Vaughnny...! I'm the elder in this mutherfuckin conversation and I know that you were raised to respect your mutherfuckin elders! I can't even try to attempt to disrespect the fact that my activities brought much disaster to your world as well as Langston's world. I brought chaos and destruction to that of my Son's world also. I cannot erase this, and nor shall I try to... but with all due respect to all that fucked up and unfortunate truth... Get you fuckin head out your sweet little fuckin ass. I have been gone and I try to keep it that way because I know I keep death four steps behind me and on each side. These fuckin women were snatched out of our neighborhood! Since you got some nuts now, your fuckin community! On your watch bitch! Not mine. All facts brother. Since you are calling the shots now, or soon to be the one calling the shots for the neighborhood. But since we don't have time for this bullshit when matters of life or death are most critical. I suggest you shut the fuck up, respect me for who the fuck I am to you, and disconnect this disrespectful tone you address me with while getting your mind right by focusing on the larger picture at hand. Leave the matter of your beloved parents and the circumstances of their untimely loss to me and your Uncle, my Brother Khaleel. Whom I knew before you were squirted out. So, we can handle matters of today and tomorrow! Nephew! How about let us start this by doing that!"

There was a chilling silence over the phone for quite some time. Langston looked awkwardly into that of Taylor's eyes,

Taylor looked questionably back into Langston's eyes. Eventually after so many gestures of visible uneasiness the two young men peered back into the rear cockpit to hopefully find some degree of what to think about the exchange in total from Denard who was oddly enough leaned back into the leather seat with his legs crossed nonchalantly over the other shocked almost in disbelief to find the two of them staring back at him for any glimpse of emotional or intellectual direction on the set of matters previously discussed or berated, whichever one either of them would choose to identify with. When suddenly out of the menacing silence came Vaughn's voice.

"Fuck you Uncle Deny! Fuck you. How is that for respect? Yeah, no doubt though, you and K can finish that conversation indeed. Hopefully face to face. Hopefully where I can see this shit. Because he is more pissed than I am about the whole fucked up situation. For the record though, I'm down with T on anything he does, even the shit I strongly disagree with, and advise against. Your slick ass mouth does make a good point. This just as much of a slap in our face as it is a continuation of your disastrous collateral damage ass coming back around. I wasn't playing. I got the whole city tooled up knowing full well that before you're off again we have some serious action on our hands. That's what you are. So, what the fuck y'all need from us? Let's just skip to that part, since everything is all rush rush rush."

This time before Taylor got himself positioned to respond he glanced back at his father to be sure he wouldn't have been interrupted again. Denard simply looked away from his son at the same moment they obtained eye contact as he gestured his hand in a wave of the hand away from his own body. With Taylor taking a distinct understanding in the silent assortment of body language from his father, he began to speak to Vaughn through the vehicle's sound system. but before he did so, he tapped Langston on the knee and touched his phone to the navigation display screen. Suddenly a GPS directional course of travel appeared. As Langston commenced to follow the directions laid out on the display Taylor began to speak with Vaughn.

"You good bro? got all that bitch shit off your chest? Ready to handle some business for me yet?", chided Taylor.

"Stop playing with me Spank. You already know how I am standing on that over here man. What the hell do you need from my life right now?", Vaugh sharply responded.

"I'm on my way to see one of your guys. Actually, he is one of

Manny's guys. We think he has a lot to do with two, if not five of the missing twenty women. Ronald is also linked to an Efren

Hernandez, who is also connected to two out of that same twenty. However, what I need from you at this moment is Information and if possible, a collection of a third person of high interest who is also linked to both these men and a fifth woman. His name is

Theodore Wright. We are heading to a warehouse on the edge of VA where both Ronald and Efren work tonight. We will hopefully have them shortly with us. We plan to meet up with you at one of my satellites by Foggy Bottoms. There will be a more appropriate location to get some much-needed intimacy with the three of them. Individually as well as potentially getting each of them in the same room. That's a big ask being short on time. I just know you're capable of making that happen. I wouldn't be surprised if you beat us there. Coordinate that with Geno."

Langston had just reached the top of the block as he turned into the neighborhood making his way to the expressway. Shortly after making his turn out following the GPS instructions, that vehicle that had been patiently waiting inconspicuously took a minute or so, but it's ignition charged on, and after its lights turned on with the engine's awakening started to proceed in following as far behind the vehicle as possible without being noticed.

As the armored, and heavily tinted black on black SUV travelled along its predetermined course across the fourteenth street bridge, and across the Potomac River made progress on its route the men within it strategized their conversations and assumed identities for the job at hand. After a few rounds of conversation and about thirty minutes of driving they had arrived at the parking lot of

their destination. The Brandmaxx distribution warehouse facility...

CHAPTER 9

"Spot Blown"

As the Three of them sat in the parking lot, Taylor and Denard both analyzed the general area and their conversations to gain entry to the facility. Denard who was first-hand familiar with most of the technology available to both himself and his illustrious brother. He spoke to the computer system within the vehicle.

"Vehicle?"

"Yes Mr. Taylor?", responded back from the vehicle's speaker system.

"From your inventory, please produce three sets of Field ready contact interface units. Then three sets of earbud communication devices", Responded Denard back to the Vehicle.

Then from the center console a dim light shone, and the six sets of small jars emerged. In between them a small plastic bottle of a substance best described as a visine like product. First, Denard took all three sets of earbud Jars and gave them to both Langston and Taylor. Denard then demonstrated how to put them into the ear by putting his set into his. Denard then took one of the other three pairs, and the eye drops. He briefly demonstrated how to insert the contact shaped objects into each eye for Taylor and Langston. When he was finished, he looked at his son and nephew, waved his hands gesturing that the process was done and complete, gesturing for them both to do the same.

"So, you want me to put those in my eyes as well Pops?", bellowed Taylor.

After a very brief bout of hesitation, with a resemblance of reluctance he gave one last look of unwillingness, Taylor followed the example led by his father in inserting the plastic objects under the lids of both of his eyes. When Taylor had completed the task with both objects, he sarcastically mocked the waving hand gesture of his father symbolizing that he had finished also.

"Happy now? Anything else Pops?" snarled Taylor.

"Actually yes, there are a few things left I need for both of you to do. One of them is to blink both of your eyes quickly." Denard responded smugly.

When Taylor did indeed "blink" his eyes he was sent back into the cushion of his seat from his initial shock to how the optical interface was initiating its startup protocols before his eyes. Langston was pushed back into his seat at this time as well, just silent. Through it a series of images ran across his view canvas. What startled him was the audible clarity to his ear buds. It wasn't loud but stereophonically complete. Taylor and Langston were both in complete awe of what the ocular devices were revealing to their senses over the environment around them. "Now softly mumble to yourselves the word 'tactical', and see what happens. Learn to play with how soft you can mumble where your words are still captured by the system.", Uttered Denard.

As the both of them took about fifteen minutes to explore their imagination with commands, to see what their ocular devices could do in result. Denard Spoke into the names of the men they came to see. He then spoke the name of the individual's name provided to him by Demetrius as their point of contact. The plant manager, Toby Finnigan. Once he had an understanding of where everyone of interest was situated within the facility. After about twenty additional minutes, Denard started to grab the door handle, and then he opened his rear passenger door. Stood there and tapped on the front passenger door where Taylor had been sitting, and spoke...

"Taylor. We need to get moving inside."

Taylor looked up at his father, and opened his door. Once out, they both straightened their clothing before walking towards the door.

"We will introduce ourselves, have the predetermined conversation explaining the purpose of our visit, and then we will take the tour. On that tour, as we run into the men highlighted on our view screens, we randomly stop asking for their opinions and notify the chaperone of our tour that we want to speak with them as well to ascertain what they've been trained on regarding the everyday practices of their departments. Once we get them alone, we can begin to speak on more direct matters. From there we request to speak outside for some fresh air. At that time Langston will reconvene so we can collect them and depart the area where we can really begin to extract the information and assistance from them that we will require. This is the plan."

Meanwhile, as Denard and Taylor continued to walk into the building, much further up the road that led to the facility is where that vehicle had parked. The vehicle that had been following the three men since they departed from Demetrius's residence. Shortly after this vehicle came to a stop, its occupant pulled out a mobile device and dialed into its number. With the device to the mysterious man's head as he seemingly placed a call and stood patiently waiting for the other end to pick up the line.

So, as Denard and Taylor entered the building, they were greeted at the employee entrance by a member of the administrative team. Susan Stidham. She had asked the men who they were, and what their business was at the facility. Denard took the authoritative posture, and introduced himself as Stanley Newman. He then introduced Taylor as James Higgins. Denard continued to explain that Scott from the corporate office sent an email to Eric describing their purpose and what we will need from onsite personnel.

"Well Eric, Mr. Welm Schiff is not present. The operations manager on shift tonight is Peter Duncan. Perhaps he will have knowledge of your expected visit. Without this we will not allow you and your associate access to the facility.", Susan said sternly, in a moderately polite tone.

"Well, we have travelled from Pennsylvania for this, and we were told that confirmation had been verified in the expectation of our arrival, so please reach out to Peter and let's hopefully determine how we can move forward here. We will only need about twenty or thirty minutes in the facility.", responded Denard.

Within about five to about eight minutes, a man emerged to the reception area through a different entryway. Soon after he greeted Susan, and she departed through that same door he introduced himself as Peter. He apologized for the misunderstandings.

"I totally forgot that you guys were coming tonight. It has been somewhat busy across all four shifts this week. I have temporary badges for the both of you. These badges will grant you access everywhere we will be tonight. I again got the email and it didn't tell me much but that Eric needed me to give you guys what you needed, and a terminal with access.", Said Peter inquisitively enough.

"Well Pete, may I call you Pete? is that acceptable for you?" asked Denard.

"Sure, no problem Mr. Newman, not a problem. Do you mind if I refer to you as Stan or Stanley?", retorted Peter.

"Sure Pete! Either works well for me to be honest", bellowed Denard.

"Well Pete, we are here to speak with you, and some random staff associates, with the potential of some front-line management to ascertain the efficacy of what has been trained to this point. We need to observe some facility operations, then utilize a terminal to log in our findings and file a report. After this we will be on or way.", Denard spoke with confident reassurance.

"Ok. Well, any one of these terminals should enable you to accomplish that. I am available if you wish to speak to me first or when you're finished inside the facility. Here is one of the mobile phones we utilize to communicate beyond radio. My name is already programmed into my number. I will leave you with one of my managers in training, Bobby for the walk around tour." Pete responded.

Taylor pulled out his pad, then began to work on the computer terminal as Denard evaluated the phone, and badges given to him from Pete. Not long after that the two of them took the badges provided and secured them to the belt loops on their pants. Once the badges were secured Denard focused his ocular device to the targets before venturing into the facility, following Bobby's lead.

With both devices synchronized to one another and connected to Langston's device who was outside in the parking lot becoming antsy, trying to postpone a bathroom break at the moment. Langston was reluctant to be caught off task doing all things relieving himself. Several images were shooting across their visual displays as they were being led around the facility. It was taking a while before his display had indicated that either men of interest had been remotely close to their position, so Denard decided to call an audible and pull Bobby to the side and ask him who a random associate walking towards their path had been.

"This guy? This is one of our crew leaders in the shipping department. This is Randall. do you want to start with him?", asked Bobby.

"Ok. Let us finish the tour and you can call him up to the office at that time.", Denard said in response.

Bobby nodded his head in agreement and continued to lead them along the back side of the warehouse. As they came around a corner both Denard and Taylor's visual displays lit up. Just about forty feet before them they could see two men conversing and from the readout on their displays those men were indeed Ronald and Efren.

Meanwhile, back at the top of the road where the vehicle that had been following the men to the facility had been parked. A new vehicle had arrived. The same oddly wrapped SUV from back near Demetrius building had pulled up alongside the vehicle. Inside of the SUV was the same rather stocky and brolic bearded gentlemen from earlier. He steps outside of the SUV and walks over to the parked sedan, and the gentlemen begin to communicate with the occupant of the vehicle. The occupant stretched his hand and arm from outside of the vehicle's window and began to point down the road towards the warehouse facility. The muscular gentlemen calmly stood erect and took a few steps away from the parked vehicle, but towards the road leading to the facility as if to look introspectively in that direction, then in each direction around the facility itself. his gaze honed in on the general direction near the facility where Colin had the vehicle parked.

At this time Colin had given into his distraction and was stepping outside of the SUV he was to find a spot to urinate quickly so he could get back on post. He had no idea their position was compromised, nor what to do about it; he had known their perimeter was breached. The SUV was armored so stepped out and took about a twenty-foot hike away from the building and the vehicle. to handle his personal business. By this time the muscular gentlemen had navigated his way just shy of about sixty yards from the vehicle's position and about seventy-five yards away from where Colin had been.

The gentlemen had been carrying a sleek, but long case along with him as he traversed the area. He finally knelt down, and carefully unclasped each section of the case that needed unclasping. Once complete, he lifted the case section upward. Inside the case was a unique looking variant of the RPG rocket launcher system. As the enigmatic stranger pulled the weapon from its casing, then ran his fingers through the case counting the additional ammunition stored with it as he loaded the tube and locked the firing mechanism into place as he squared his broad shoulders and fixated on his target. The vehicle was in between Langston and the curious gentleman.

What Langston was not aware of was that the SUV he had driven in was coated in a material similar to the material used by snipers in the field that mask temperature. Where in the case of the stealthy sniper it would prevent anyone from detecting their presence. In this case, the coating prevents the heat from within the cockpit or more importantly that from its engine from being detected. Langston's SUV was heavily armored and virtually indestructible under normal circumstances. There had not been any field testing for how it's armor would withstand or fail to the blast of an RPG round.

The mysterious man with the rocket nonchalantly fired one off in the direction of Langston and his SUV. The round made contact with the ground just underneath the vehicle. The blast caused the vehicle to flip violently back from its original position, however tumbling towards Langston. The deafening sound from the blast stole every idea of Langston's' attention while shocking him. That shock saved his life where it inspired him to duck and turn around. As he did so the vehicle came flying by him slightly over his body. but the door he had left ajar swung around and caught his torso with enough force to immediately knock him unconscious on the ground somewhat under the SUV where it landed. He was unconscious but otherwise unharmed.

At the same exact time within the facility, the blast was quite loud and irregular to the typical sounds heard there. As a result, people did stop to look around and check their surroundings but overall, nothing was done about it and as it disappeared the facility continued to return to normal operations since it was considered an isolated incident. However, Denard and Taylor were not so swayed. Especially Denard. Denard instructed his ocular device to perform a security sweep of the area to include a patch to Langston's ocular device to enhance the coverage area in the hopes of seeing what the aftermath of that sound had left in its wake.

"Mr. Higgins, I believe we have a situation developing outside.", whispered Denard.

"Excuse me? What did you just say?", answered Taylor inquisitively in a whisper of his own.

Immediately Taylor grew concerned for the welfare of his younger cousin just outside. There solely because he was following him in the abyss.

"I cannot establish a link with Langston's ocular device. Which could mean one of two things; Either he is passed out or dead. Either way that is no good. We need to secure these two now, and get out there to him immediately!", Denard whispered back more sternly.

Denard grabbed Bobby at the shoulder, and brought their bodies closer to one another so he could speak to him.

"These two will do fine. This place has a lot going on tonight. perhaps it was poorly coordinated. Let's wrap this up. If what we develop is not satisfactory, then we will just have to set an additional date to do so. For now, bring those two with you back to the office." commanded Denard.

Just as Denard spoke his words into the ear of the manager in training, Bobby began to act upon them. He walked over to Efren and Ronald. Ronald took a second look at Taylor and recognized him slightly. He grew hesitant because he knew his name was not James as told to him by Bobby. His next move was to inconspicuously get the attention of Efren and have him look to confirm his suspicion in recognizing Taylor. Efren did also.

Unsure what was really taking place, Ronald copied because what he did know was even though he wasn't completely sure who Taylor was he knew he had only recognized him in connection to his dealings with Manny. Recalling this, he suddenly became aware that there wasn't much running from Manny, so it was a better choice to follow along with the charade until he could figure out what this was all about.

As the three men began to walk away... Denard and Taylor followed close behind. Both Taylor and his father were immediately distracted from the awkward readout coming across the visual display of their devices. Still all new to Taylor what symbols meant what, he was still distracted long after Denard had already grabbed him by the arm, along with two hard hats as they passed through the maintenance tunnel and started to run.

Grabbing both Ronald and Efren along their way.

"This spot is about to get some serious air conditioning! Run! Now!" Yelled Denard.

Just like that. A second blast had now struck the wall of the facility. Causing massive destruction within the facility. This blast was followed by a third, and a fourth blast. All three blasts decimated the structure. Without a doubt the vents of the explosion took the lives of nearly eighty six percent of all its inhabitants.

The blast radius could easily be seen across the Potomac River. As a matter of fact, Demetrius noticed the blast immediately across his balcony. Where he could not avoid the widening of his eyes just before he initiated the shutters to close off the view from the balcony. His next move was to summon his assistant discreetly.

When she arrived, he leaned into her ear and whispered to her.

"Get my response teams out to that facility that just blew the fuck up immediately! Get my Brother and my nephews out of there before all hell goes loose over there with the media and law enforcement. ASAP!", whispered Demetrius.

Then Demetrius went back to conversing with his dinner guests.

While the building was still smoldering from the rocket fire, Denard managed to maintain a grip on his Son, Taylor was able to maintain a grip on both Efren and Ronald. They had managed to make it to a structurally reinforced area of the building. There was no trace of the mysterious gentleman who besieged the facility in less than ten minutes. Still completely covered in soot, Denard arose from the collection of dust and debris with his Son in grip.

Taylor arose barely holding onto Efren and Ronald who were still gasping for air and fighting the loss of awareness. The two people of interest were borderline incoherent and unconscious as they were pulled to the area of the wreckage that was formerly the front of the building. Literally just moments before.

"Where is Langston?", asked Taylor aloud.

Denard put each of his hands across the shoulders of both Ronald and Efren as Taylor went ahead to search for his younger cousin feverishly, and with increasing desperation. Once away from immediate wreckage surrounding the building's location Taylor could see the SUV undamaged but on its side off and up the hill along the wooded trail of the parking lot perimeter. He then instructed his ocular device as it flickered in and out of normal operational functionality to search for Langston's heat signature. As he arrived at the vehicle, he searched through it calling for his cousin as he reached and pulled branches out of the vehicle's cockpit. He sat on the ground momentarily in despair, as he started to entertain the grim reality that he may have just lost another close family member and this time a long-standing friend also.

"I see his signature.", Yelled Denard from back down the hill

"He is up about ten yards from your location. He is on the ground under the vehicle's propped open door that is dug into the ground above.", Denard continued to yell.

As Taylor hurried to search the location near the truck his father had directed him to, the response unit that Demetrius had sent out for them had just arrived. Their vehicle stopped and quickly quite a few individuals rushed from within it and made haste towards the same location Taylor was just arriving at himself. As Taylor arrived, he found his younger cousin unconscious, and lying peacefully on the ground just beneath the door. The response unit members grabbed a hold of Langston and carefully dragged him from his position and carted him off with them precisely. Then the next set of their team attached a hook to the chassis of their SUV, and gave a hand signal to the team members still by the vehicle they arrived in and the wench attached to the hook pulled the vehicle back upright and down the hill. Due to the vehicle's extreme rigid construction, the only damage sustained was some minor denting. It started up immediately once its ignition had been engaged.

Denard took a very distraught Efren and Ronald towards the rear of their SUV, and zip tied them appropriately before ushering them into the rear cockpit of the vehicle. Denard then went to the driver's side of the SUV and began to open a panel on the side of the set and began to input a series of commands into the keyboard in the panel. Then suddenly the vehicle responded to those commands by reconfiguring its rear passenger layout. A cage bar rolled up from the floor board up behind the front seats between where he and Taylor would sit and their two passengers were strapped in.

Denard then initiated a systems analysis, which took a few minutes, but came back successful, displaying operational functionality status detected on the screen read out. A member of the response unit came up to the driver's side door just behind Denard and informed him that they have secured an alternate route away from the incident. Denard then called out to Taylor.

"Son! Come to the truck. We have to leave now."

"Where are they taking Langston?", asked Taylor in response.

"Demetrius sent these people to assist us, so wherever Langston is being taken he will certainly be safe.", Denard responded.

Slightly comforted by hearing the response of his father, Taylor jumped into the vehicle as best he was able considering still having some soreness from the wreckage. Denard also demonstrated some degree of struggle as he too entered the vehicle. As their vehicle began to move forward and behind the response unit SUV, they began down a different path towards the other side of the facility heading east instead of north like they came in. Eventually they arrived on the river bank where there were amphibious mini barges awaiting both vehicles. Once secured atop each of them they were raced across the Potomac as the race of several law enforcement vehicles raced across the three ninety-five along the Arland D. Williams, Jr. Memorial Bridge.

With their convoy speeding across, Denard was attempting to get

Demetrius on the phone. Whereas Demetrius was just escorting the ladies from dinner out to his car service staff. Once the ladies had been placed into their vehicle, and their driver taking off, Demetrius called his brother back as he quickly moved back into his building. Along the way he called Arthur on his hand-held radio and informed him that the current security status of the property needed to be placed on high alert.

"What happened out there?" inquired Demetrius.

"I wish I actually knew man. We had both Ronald and Efren in our custody then the building blew up from what seemed as the result of multiple RPG's fired into the building.", Denard replied.

"Well, the recognizance vehicle is still intact, correct? Perhaps its system gathered some details of what took place before it was blown up that hill. Get it back to the building and park it on the deck with my Utility van you had just used. We will connect their systems and see what information is there.", Replied Demetrius.

As both barges traveled southbound towards their rendezvous location at Fox Ferry Point. They travelled as inconspicuous as possible slipping beyond visibility past Bolling Air Force Base without obtaining any unwanted attention from their aquatic security force units. Upon their arrival at Fox Ferry. The response unit barge took to ground first, then assisted the barge carrying Denard, Taylor, Ronald and Efren in doing the me. There was a tractor trailer that had an empty storage container awaiting their arrival. Once both SUVs were taken off the barges, and both barges brought successfully on land, a technician from inside the big rig came out and began to input commands into the side panel of both barges in addition to a hand-held unit he possessed. As a result of his actions the barges began to move through a series of automated controls. When these maneuvers had completed the set of barges were now small enough to fit into the empty container. Then with the same handheld device the technician controlled the mini crane installed at the rear of the truck's cabin, loading the container onto the rear of the rig. After that process was complete, and the technician re-entered the cockpit of the truck, He took the Trailer and disappeared into the evening. Both SUVs did the same enroute to Demetrius's building.

There was much concern as they travelled to Demetrius's residence and virtual safe house. Neither Taylor or Denard at that time knew exactly how their position had been compromised or by who. So, the threat was still out there as far as Denard was concerned. Reaching the safe house was of the utmost importance. Once they crossed back into the District of Columbia Demetrius also recognizing the same threat assessment made a few calls, and before their convoy reached the Anacostia Freeway

A special tactical security force unit had been dispatched from Bolling Air Force base ironically enough.

"What the hell do you want from us man?", Wined Ronald from the rear of the vehicle with Efren frantically nodding his head in agreement.

"Oh! I just about forgot that the two of you guys were back there.

You both might want to shut each of ya mouths. Obviously neither of y'all built for what you're seeing. So, sit tight, and when we get to the part where what we need from you both is at hand then your best option is to tell us what we ask for... completely." Scowled Denard back at them.

Both men took to silence immediately after Denard had spoken. distracted by the flashing lights of their military escort convoy. Then after they made some considerable distance on the freeway more municipal law enforcement joined their escort team. Both men realized that despite neither of them knowing much about what was taking place, they did accept the fact that these men transporting them had far too much military and law enforcement for them to handle by themselves. Not to disregard that Ronald recognized Taylor as being the nephew of Khaleel. Who was the boss of his boss Manny. Manny scared him to anxiety all by himself. At the end of it all he realized that complying was in their best interest.

Before long the vehicles were approaching the Navy Yard bridge. As they crossed the bridge Taylor was still quite consumed with the status of Langston's health predicament. Let alone being the person who'd have to convey his health status to his older brother Vaughn who never approved of his involvement in these affairs to begin with. Without any doubt in his mind, he knew he was going to be the recipient of Vaughn's outrage over the situation of his younger brother's health condition whatever it may be at this point. Taylor continued to struggle with his involvement in encouraging Langston's participation in his dealings with the new endeavors taken on with his Father and Uncle.

Taylor glared off overlooking the communities that comprised his neighborhood in whole as they raced to his Uncle's residence. A place where he spent the majority of his childhood. They came upon the top of the road that led to the cul de sac where

Demetrius residence stood. As they approached the building it was apparent that there was a significant increase in the visibility of the security forces on duty at the residence property. As they made their way up into the parking structure, they first encountered Arthur who redirected their travel to the area where they initiated their investigation back next to the utility van belonging to Demetrius and the smaller van belonging to Taylor's team.

Waiting for them both, standing between the vans was Demetrius. He was displeased at best from the expression on his face, but definitely much more relieved to see the two of them again. As their vehicles came to a stop, the men that were once inside stepped out the vehicle almost simultaneously and approached both rear passenger doors on Taylor and Denard's Vehicle, opened its doors then unsecured both Ronald and Efren from their restraints and brought them into the building. Denard and Demetrius embraced one another first as Denard exited the vehicle and walked over to his brother.

"Would you care to tell me what in the hell happened out there? you were only supposed to get those two and bring them back.

How did things go so wrong Deny?", questioned Demetrius. "Demetrius, I already told you. I barely know myself. I was fortunate enough to receive the display readout when I did the incoming RPG fire. Then, all hell you referred to just broke loose. All I was thinking about was Langston, and what he had going on while all this was taking place. I was grateful we found him and his vitals were still strong despite being unconscious.", replied

Denard

Then Taylor, before completely exiting the vehicle, took a moment to gather his thoughts. Mostly regarding his concern for Langston, then growing extremely curious about how Langston even got hurt in the first place. Taylor then exited the vehicle and approached both his Father and Uncle where they stood between the vans.

"I'm glad that you're a one-piece nephew. I know that you are concerned about Langston. Just as we are. I had him brought to my medical services office. You know where that is. So, when we are done here you go see him then or you can go now. That's totally up to you."

Taylor took the option to be by his cousin's side and departed quickly into the building. At this point Denard and Demetrius both entered into the larger utility van. Denard entering first as Demetrius lingered behind him to instruct Arthur.

"Have our reconnaissance vehicle connected through the data interface please. Then start its ignition and man its cockpit. We will coordinate our commands from there with one another.", ordered Demetrius to Arthur.

"Yes Sir.", responded Arthur.

Once the two vehicles were connected and the data transfer link was successfully established. Demetrius began to bridge the security protocols of the SUV to access the surveillance imagery within its files. Quickly enough since Demetrius possessed all the required credentials to access the database, he was able to start looking through the files on the vehicle's hard drive. Once he reached the folder system for the footage recorded moments to the incident. Demetrius pointed out to Denard something he recognized as odd.

"Do you see that blip coming in from the north of the facility's property? look here at this location." instructed Demetrius.

"I do see that. It looks to me like a vehicle. Then alongside of is a moving object that appears to also be a vehicle, but its visual display seems very much different. Actually, it looks similar to what our vehicle heat signature technology would look like under the same scrutiny." Responded Denard.

"Agreed. I was thinking along the same line. So, I have a filter that recognizes this technology as it blocks the presence of heat as it is dispersed. However, it focuses the sensors into isolating the heat in a comparative analysis to its environment. The heat patterns should be consistent with its given environment. So, we can still track heat based on those parameters." retorted Demetrius.

The wall of displays began to populate files. So, Demetrius picked the file folder labeled 'perimeter check' from the list of folders. Within that folder were a set of spreadsheet files and video files with coordinating files names. Denard selected the filename amongst the video sets he felt was closest to just before his recollection of the initial impact. He chose the filename that coincided with when he and Taylor first heard the initial blast. As the video file loaded into the program in process to display its images both Demetrius and Denard were distraught when they could see clear as day the two vehicles arriving just about sixty yards from where Langston should have been by the vehicle if not inside of it.

"Where's Langston while these guys are approaching his location?", asked Demetrius.

"He was supposed to be in the truck the whole time monitoring the surveillance systems Demetrius. This is news to me." Denard responded back confused.

Then Demetrius pulled up an additional window and sent its data to one of the several screens along the workstations wall unit. He pulled up a file labeled 'rotating three sixty view' for the time frame coinciding with the perimeter check file that was being watched on the main screen display. It wasn't long after doing so they could both easily see Langston walking away from the truck to about twenty yards south of its location to what appeared to be him urinating. It was at this time that from the two unknown vehicles a person emerged from the foggy imagery into focus with a long, sleek briefcase at his side. Shortly after seeing this person walk calmly in the direction of the SUV where Langston should have been sitting attentively inside, he knelt down and opened his sleek case to unharness an advanced RPG rocket firing device. This person took aim at the SUV which was difficult for both of them to watch and the final moments of footage was observing the RPG fire its rocket at the vehicle, and the vehicle obviously flipping over several times. There was a vague section of footage where it could be seen how and where the vehicle's open door struck Langston hard enough to knock him out, while clean enough to leave him minimally damaged. With that mystery somewhat laid to rest and uncovered. The men drew their focuses back onto those few moments before the mysterious assailant fired his weapon to where a facial image was captured.

"Denard, do you recognize this guy?" asked Demetrius hesitantly.

"I hope I am seeing a ghost at the moment. But I think I have seen that person before. Let's hope that I am incorrect. Let's see what

Cosmos produces before I jump to any rash conclusions Demetrius." responded Denard with much reluctance.

Cosmos made a positive identification verification within seven minutes of internal processing through a litany of global security networks. Interpol, Langley, and more agencies that operate around the European, Middle Eastern, and Asian political and intelligence community. On the main screen displayed a face.

Much clearer than the one captured in the perimeter scan video.

The face was definitely the same as the one on the video however, with the additional detail Denard was forced to stand from his seated position and turn around in displeasure. Demetrius immediately took notice of this, and grew displeased himself.

"So, you definitely know this man Denard? Come out with it! We don't have time for this shit man. who the hell is this guy?", Demetrius scowled at his younger brother.

Then growing more than just impatient with the delay in his expected response from his brother, Demetrius turned his focus to Cosmos for assistance.

"Cosmos? search every municipal camera and cctv system in the state for this face after it is catalogued into facial recognition. I want to know whenever he's popped up on the system!

Immediately!" scowled Demetrius again.

"Yes, Delegate Fortune", responded Cosmos.

Demetrius turned back to his brother and spoke harshly once again.

"Tell me who this person is Denard!", berated Demetrius

"His name is Faddei Kalashik. he is far more well known as and referred to as 'жестокий' or the 'Cruel One'. He is an accomplished and decorated mercenary of Russian descent. He has worked for many governments however; his previous assignments have earned him a significant and profoundly diverse legion of supporters across the region. There are few who would defy him. He can definitely pose a serious problem. His presence here is connected without question to my ongoing issues with that individual we are aware of from that original file. They have never stopped their pursuit for revenge. This latest attempt was more of a message. Me and Kalashik have a history of our own. He wants me to know about his contract so we can conduct this challenge in a more suitable format. It is me he is after. I have to leave now to avoid this from affecting any of you and finally ending this conflict once and for all. First I will deal with Kalashik then his employer." Denard confessed to Demetrius.

Denard, still standing, said one last thing to his brother.

"Give my son the assistance he needs to do better than I have with this. I accepted long ago that some greatness comes at great costs.

I can no longer postpone the inevitability of these past endeavors. I must handle this old business now. Watch over my son like you have done so for just about his whole life. He will need you even more now Brother. Please."

The Denard walked out of the vehicle, and disappeared into the night by the time Demetrius was able to follow behind him, to even get to say goodbye or see you soon.

CHAPTER 10

"Chain Reaction"

Demetrius sat and went through every byte of data obtained from the reconnaissance vehicle. He was able to get the license plate information for both vehicles after an intensive search utilizing several satellite arrays. His governmental access and contacts for deeper system penetration were his sole allies in the search with the exception to the analytical prowess of Cosmos. During this time Demetrius also examined all the documentation that Denard and Taylor had at their disposal before they departed to the facility. This information included Cosmos's findings that led them to Ronald, Efren, and Theodore Wright. Demetrius further examined each dossier on all three men. He additionally delved deeper into each background for each woman labeled as missing in the original file.

Demetrius was well aware of how distracting the injury to Langston would pose onto Taylor. This he acknowledged was not how he wanted this chapter to start for him. The threat that these events pose to his community were too ambiguous to render an absolute plan towards a solution. The involvement of that random mercenary comfortable enough to operate with such impunity within his governmental jurisdiction stung Demetrius in a place he could not scratch or reach. disturbing him deeply. Demetrius now riveted in serious contemplation and strategic evaluation of his options, reached within his sports coat and pulled out a long magnificent looking cigar. Clipped its tip, and then began to ignite its proper end as he inhaled upon its other end methodically. With his legs crossed, and his posture leaned back into the leather chair he just thought as he sat.

"Where did my father go Uncle D?", asked Taylor suddenly.

Startled as much as it was to be possible for Demetrius, he jumped slightly in his seat, as he was definitely not expecting Taylor at that moment.

"Your father recognized the image provided by the vehicle you guys were in the surveillance system. The man he recognized was associated with past dealings of your father. He was devastated that yet again his past dealings caused the injury of a family member here at home. So, he went off to deal with that situation once and for all."

"I expect that we will see him again. Just as your mother inspires you, and her sister and late husband also inspire Langston, Vaughn and Khaleel... He is even more inspired to exact his revenge on anyone connected to that chapter of his. His resiliency and diligence are unmatched." Continued Demetrius.

"So, I expect to see your father again. I hope to see the peace in his face when he has accomplished his goal."

Taylor stood still for a few moments. He looked back out from the entryway of the vehicle into the abyss of the parking structure.

After a decent amount of time doing so he turned back to his Uncle

"So, it's me and you right now?", Asked Taylor.

"Just about Nephew. For the time being.", responded Demetrius.

Again, Taylor took additional time to hold back his initial reaction, as he was obviously experiencing a difficult emotional moment internally. This demonstration was more visibly difficult for Demetrius to watch than the original one. Suddenly, Taylor turned to his Uncle with a blank stare to say,

"So, let's handle our business Unc. Let's do what we need to get done." Taylor said with a resolute voice.

"Well Nephew, I have gone through all of this data at least four times. We need to speak to the two you guys brought in and see what additional information we can extract from them."

Demetrius called to Arthur who had still been in the SUV. told him to relocate all three vehicles and secure them.

"Arthur, lock down this facility."

Once Arthur set off to complete the task, Demetrius and Taylor hurried into the building. Ronald and Efren were now sitting inside of an auxiliary conference room with four security specialists that worked for the Delegate. Efren was obviously leaning on Ronald for direction in these matters. Efren was completely out of his element and quite frightened. Ronald was not far from where Efren was emotionally but he did have some degree of security knowing that he has some resemblance of affiliation with the people he was with. Little was he aware that his affiliation had placed him in a more complicated position than he had expected.

Taylor and Demetrius walked up to the door to the conference room, then Demetrius put his arm out in front of Taylor to stop him from entering.

"Taylor."

"Yes Unc?", Taylor impatiently responded as respectfully as he could.

"Look, I understand you're frustrated and possibly quite angry at a litany of things. Denard just left, Langston is unconscious, and we still don't have much new information where these women are. However, be careful not to lose track of our purpose. Be careful not to confuse one situation with another. These men here have nothing to do with Your father or Langston. The individual responsible for most of this is unfortunately my brother. Although he was just doing what he was assigned to do, at high success, he just had to pay the unfortunate price that comes from what he does primarily. Some in the field get the blowback more than others. He has received much blowback in many areas of his life. Tonight, was more of that pattern playing itself out. Somewhere in there lies my accountability. I am well aware of the reality of the wave of collateral damage that follows my brother everywhere he has been for the last twenty plus years. What we need to focus on for this moment is that these two men have potentially something to do with the disappearances of at least four women that we can surmise. Extracting as much new information from them as to their relationships with these women, and what they may or may not know about bringing these women back as quickly as possible has to be our sole focus. My specialist, Daniel will lead this interrogation. My face is far too easily recognized for me to be hands on with this type of activity. Feel free to pace around, listening, and learning how they conduct themselves. Watch for any facial reactions and body language. Here is where you bring your talent in understanding people to the table. Now go and learn so eventually you will be capable of doing this on your own well,

Nephew."

Taylor nodded his head, and then Demetrius's specialist walked out of a different door where he had been waiting for Demetrius to arrive for the interrogation to begin.

"Taylor, this is our specialist in these types of interrogations. His name is Daniel."

Taylor and Daniel shook hands briefly, and then entered the conference room together. As they entered the room, Ronald grew attentive to the opportunity of hopefully talking himself, and hopefully Efren out of this predicament. Whereas Efren was reluctant to establish, or maintain any kind of eye contact with either the seasoned specialist or Taylor. Seeing this, Daniel began speaking to Ronald while he paced around, and staring at Efren with the sole intention of hoping to keep Efren intimidated but not afraid.

"Ronald... I need some information from you. Will you give me this information?" Spoke Daniel in an eerie tone.

"What is it that you need to know Sir? I do not understand why I am here. I do not understand why that building exploded when this man came to get me with the other man either. we barely escaped with our lives. At this point I just want for us to go home. If I know something that you want or need to know I sure want to tell you what that is." responded Ronald.

The specialist Stood still, and then leaned over the table with his hands planted on its edge. As he did these things he spoke again, as his tone transitioned from eerie to disturbingly creepy.

"This pleases me for the moment. You both I can imagine want to go back to the normalcy of your individual lives. I can relate. If this is what you truly want Ronald, then you will do as you have said you will do. You will answer each question I ask, thoroughly, and complete in every sense of the subject matter. To be safe (awkward emphasis placed on the annunciation of this word), You may want to skip to the part where once I ask you a question, that you will tell me everything you know on that subject, and I will decide what part, if not the whole of it is what I need from you on that subject. If you were to be smart about it. To be fair, this is my advice for both of you."

To this, Efren began to grow more frantic. It was becoming obvious that the two of them had agreed for Ronald to do most if not all of the talking in these matters. So, now that Daniel has brought the conversation to a place where there is a definite potential for negative outcomes if the information provided is interpreted as unsatisfactory. Efren was visibly quite uncomfortable about having to now potentially suffer the unknown negative consequence from Ronald's choices in responses. Daniel saw this, and continued to stoke the fire of unease.

"Efren... no, excuse me... Ronald, I will start by giving you an opportunity to impress me and give me a sense of reward in having you succeed in responding to this question beyond my expectations... Do you have a romantic relationship with Mrs.

Noreen Martin?", asked Daniel.

"Yes, we were romantically involved, but that relationship ended recently.", responded Ronald with some leeriness.

"Oh, how unfortunate to hear it didn't work out. Are you two still on speaking terms? Will she take your calls still", asked Daniel.

"Yeah, for the most part. I don't know. I haven't called her since our last time speaking together.", responded Ronald.

Meanwhile Efren is increasingly exhibiting body language of a person suffering from symptoms of a pending anxiety attack on the horizon. Daniel was continuously observing Efren's unease as he began to structure the framework of his questioning of Ronald.

"Well Ronald. here is an opportunity for you to impress me and encourage my desire to be kind with the two of you... I want you to take this phone (slides the phone unit that was already sitting in the center of the conference room over to where Ronald was sitting), and I want you to call Noreen for me right now."

Ronald's body language was now starting to fluctuate into a degree of nervousness. As a direct reaction to seeing Ronald begin to lose whatever confidence he had initially shown to Efren to have him relying on his associate to speak for him effectively was beginning to erode even faster as Ronald began to exhibit signs of uncontrollable unease himself. Taylor continued to pace around the room, and periodically stand awkwardly behind Efren's seat often. Daniel pressed further as he was now sitting on the edge of the conference table awaiting Ronald to pick up the receiver and dial Noreen's telephone number into the base. The longer, and less patiently Daniel sat there giving off the feeling that his patience was wearing thinner as the minutes passed on was making Ronald more uncomfortable which in turn was making Efren increasingly more nervous as he fidgeted in his seat with the passing of each utterance from either of the two men conversing.

"It seems to me that there is a reason you must have in being so hesitant to even call Noreen. Why is this? Will you tell me why? Do I need to abandon this peaceful approach to my needs from you? Poor Efren hasn't got the opportunity to say a word here. I wonder if he is willing to be on the receiving end of your decision to be unhelpful?", Spoke Daniel with an aura of intensified authority.

Ronald, now realizing that he was going to have to make a decision shortly in regards to explaining himself. He was also becoming aware that Efren was beginning to deviate from the original plan, and it was just a matter of time before he spilled every bean he could recall. Ronald had to reevaluate his situation immediately before it turned on him took any option he may have had away with grim consequences.

"I can't call her man. She got kidnapped. I set her up to get snatched. Some guy from a friend I know was telling some of us at a bar that if we could assist them in finding ideal females for them to abduct. I needed the money man they were offering us five grand for each one man... I gave them her address and picture." Ronald frantically exclaimed.

Hearing this Efren even more petrified, blurted out finally,

"I too did the same deal with those men. I gave them two names and addresses. I told them about two women I had been seeing at the same time and got caught cheating by them both. Alissa Rodriguez, and Merita Delgado." Efren blurted out with relief to most of his anxiety.

"OK this is along the lines of what I needed to hear from the both of you. What can you tell me about Theodore Wright? WAs she present that evening at that bar where the person made the offer for the whereabouts of these women he intended to have abducted? Who is this man? Where can I find him?", Daniel continued to question.

Both Efren and Ronald at the same time without coordination jumped to say,

"Theodore was the guy. He made us the offer."

"Where can we find Mr. Wright?", Asked Daniel.

The two of them sunk into their seats when asked that question. Which was either one of two signs as Daniel saw it; Either they honestly were unsure of where he could be found, or a continual demonstration of avoiding his questions, diminishing how he could evaluate how truthfully, they've answered him.

"All I know is that he told us both stories of how he gave the same information for two of his previous exe's. If you give me the opportunity, I can show you where he had always been on Thursday evenings. Because this is where we would always see him after we took off from work to grab a couple cold ones before heading home for the night." Answered Ronald quickly.

"Well tomorrow will be Thursday. Which one of you wants to volunteer to take a trip with us to verify your claims while the other one remains here, awaiting the outcome?" Eerily asked by Daniel with an awkwardly inviting smirk on his face.

Efren jumped to claim that opportunity.

"Me, I will help you. Please allow me to help you." pleaded Efren.

Ronald was not entirely pleased with Efren as he jumped to the forefront of the situation so willingly. Despite that Ronald still felt to some degree in an advantageous position. No mention so far of his affiliation to Manny nor Khaleel and that group whatsoever. He was concerned about that more than anything. He was definitely hesitant about the possibility that Khaleel or Vaughn would stroll through the door at any moment. Then he knew he'd be acting more scared than Efren.

Ronald also knew that Efren did not run in any of the circles he had been running with over the years. They were just co-workers for the most part. It would've been much better in hindsight for Efren to take that trip because there was no telling who would have seen him in whatever vehicle they would have paraded him through the neighborhood in, and none of that would have bode well for him at all. So, considering the tentative stability of his situation in regards to his safety, he turned in his chair and offered no objection to Efren taking the trip.

Daniel took a look at Taylor to non-verbally exchange an understanding of how for the moment they were finished here. Lesson complete. Taylor wasn't exactly sure how to interpret the gesture fully. But stayed true to his Uncle's Advice on how to proceed. Daniel left the room first, then Taylor came out next.

Demetrius was standing out there waiting. He still had headphones on as he was listening along the whole time.

"You did well Daniel, Taylor I am sure you have seen something that enhanced you. I can't wait to see how you take whatever that was to the next level. I suggest you continue to follow up with Efren and Daniel on locating this Theodore Wright character, and bringing him in so we can get a crack at what he knows.", Demetrius declared.

As Demetrius finished speaking to Daniel and Taylor, Arthur pulled up in a different surveillance SUV. Daniel placed Efren into the heavily tinted and armored vehicle as he and Taylor then entered the vehicle with a fourth security specialist who joined them per the instructions of Demetrius. They also provided a security follow car group mixed in marked and unmarked distinction vehicles. Demetrius was not taking any chances with the safety of his nephew again after the events of that evening. After the SUV departed the parking deck level where Demetrius stood, he went off back into the building. He knew he had an unpleasant phone call he had to make. It was not going to be a pleasant evening as a result.

Before they took the appropriate direction that would have taken them to the bar where Theodore Wright was said to be easily found. Taylor however needed to have that itinerary deviated. He had to go see Vaughn. He was way late in reaching out once they had got Langston secured in the first place. Already aware that this notification pursuant conversation was going to be abrasive and difficult, he was devoted to the idea of making that take place immediately.

"Hey brother, I need to have this truck take a slight detour that is of equal importance to the task at hand if not greater. I will have to explain to you later in the evening once we complete the task we originally came out for. You can reach out to Delegate Fortune, and he will tell you the same thing."

Daniel looked slightly annoyed with the last-minute change to the game plan, but went along with it without saying much in dispute to the suggestion.

"Go over by the Dupont Park section of the South east. Once we get there I will get out and speak with an individual for about twenty minutes. No matter how animated the conversation becomes, leave us be. It is a personal matter of the family. I am reaching out to him via text now so he will be prepared for our arrival." Requested Taylor, politely.

Taylor texted Vaughn.

"We need to meet. We have some matters to discuss."

Vaughn responded back to Taylor within the next three minutes.

"WTF! Why is Langston not answering my calls T? Meet me by the park off Randle Circle man" Vaughn speed texted Taylor.

As the SUV whizzed through Capitol Hill on Pennsylvania Avenue, headed towards the John Philip Sousa Bridge Taylor remained silent despite the fact that he could feel the stares coming from Daniel in displeasure at having been taken off course for an unknown matter. A matter that as far as he was concerned, had nothing to do with the investigation he was assigned. The vehicle reached the thirty-two hundred blocks in Minnesota and parked. Taylor stepped out the vehicle slowly, and as he did so, suddenly from around the corner, almost immediately walked out a rather stocky built individual. The man walked quite fast into Taylor's personal space and began to speak with him from the view from inside the vehicle as if the conversation was confrontational.

"Where is my little Brother Taylor?", bellowed Vaughn aggressively.

"He was badly injured earlier this evening when we were together trying to find some information about the missing women, we were talking with you about." Taylor answered remorsefully.

"Hmmm, well where is Uncle Denard at? Wasn't he with y'all too?", Vaughn answered back still aggressively.

Taylor paused and looked distraught before he responded back.

"My pops just left town again Vaughn. It is not what you think actually but in the same line of what we already know that follows my father. He left to see it through once and for all. Langston's' injury was the last straw it seemed for him. Demetrius told me he snapped and just left without even saying goodbye, but to say he wasn't returning until he settled this matter and those keeping it an issue or he won't return." Taylor reluctantly answered back.

Vaughn was still frustrated and upset about not knowing how badly his brother had been injured, but then decided to calm down and take some positivity from hearing his Uncle finally made the move his cousin told him he set off to see through.

"So where is Langston? I want to go see him." Asked Vaughn of Taylor.

"He is at the private emergency medical center in Uncle Demetrius building. He has not regained consciousness though. He took a blow to the head in the field and although all his vitals are excellent, he was still out like a light when we left to find you and to handle another matter of business."

"Ok, I will head over there with Khaleel in a few then."

"No problem. Call Uncle Demetrius before you head out. Because of all the commotion this evening He has the whole entire building on lockdown. With us we have a guy that was an associate of

Ronald Evans, who works for your guy Manny. His Name is Efren Hernandez. He is supposed to be taking us to find another person of increased interest, Theodore Wright. Does the name mean anything to you? Have you heard that name before from anyone?" Asked Taylor.

"No, not off the rip, but I will check these things out. I will get with Khaleel and Manny too. We will figure out something. Be careful out there. I see your rolling heavy now. Y'all should have been rolling this heavy from the gate. Happy to see you're getting smarter cousins. And just so you know that I know... Langston detests taking 'L's', so a major problem started tonight, thanks to the two of you. You know he will not take any of this well.", Vaughn responded back to Taylor.

Then Vaughn took off walking back around the same corner that he came from and disappeared just as quickly as he emerged. Taylor turned back toward the SUV, reached out for the handle, pulled it back open and hopped back into the Truck.

"Ok, let's get back on the route to that bar.", Taylor said to Daniel.

Taylor was completely undeterred by the facial expression on Daniel's face of disapproval.

As they made their way to the bar located on sixth street. There was an awkward and lingering silence within the cabin of the vehicle as they approached Constitution Avenue. Daniel picked up his hand-held radio at this point and commenced to communicate with the different vehicles that comprised the convoy he was leading and managing.

"Team Four, Park your vehicle discreetly on the corner of 'Foxtrot' Street and Seventh Street' behind the Mexican restaurant at that intersection. Team Five, park near the intersection of 'Echo' Street and Seventh Street to where you can see both Seventh and 'Echo' Street, and keep visual contact with team Four. Team Four I need you to keep visual contact with Team five as well. Tactical Team two, I need for your team to park strategically between 'Echo' and 'Foxtrot' along Fifth Street. Team Three, your team needs to maintain mobility around the circumference of 'Foxtrot Street', 'Sixth Street', 'Echo Street', and 'Seventh Street'. Team One will park conspicuously along 'Sixth Street' nearest to the intersection on 'Foxtrot Street'. Security forces will remain inside the vehicle to maintain security over the Informant Tactical Team Six will maintain Satcom, and once the package is up, I want all persons of interest painted, so if we have a runner, we can track this piece of shit where it goes, then grab him if not before...Tactical team two will maintain visual line of sight on Tactical Team One vehicle due to the informant. Myself and Taylor will take a trip inside the Bar and evaluate the situation from inside. We will minimize radio contact until I say otherwise. Once." Commanded Daniel before he and Taylor exited the vehicle and began their approach to the bar's entrance.

Taylor took the initiative to enter the establishment first. He requested for Daniel to wait approximately five minutes before he came in behind him. Taylor knew that he had a different energy about him, and having been a known local figure he entered into the establishment would have produced a completely different one that of Daniel's. Also, Taylor conducted his own business in this bar on several occasions. He would have preferred not to have whatever suspicion Daniel would have brought upon himself to transfer over onto his reputation if avoidable. This is exactly how those events played out. Taylor walked into the bar with reception and approval. When Daniel came in a few minutes behind Taylor the reaction was much different. The tension within the bar had drastically changed. As if the entire bar recognized a member of law enforcement had entered the space altering the freedoms that perceptively existed before his arrival. Daniel picked up on the vibe and immediately disliked Taylor just a little more for putting him in that position without giving him the heads up.

"That smug bastard.", Daniel muttered to himself under his breath as he accepted the reality of his current predicament.

Daniel knew that with his reception his only move was to play the bar. From there he could only make visual confirmation of the person of interest and wait for his ocular device to confirm that identity. He could only assume that once he confirmed the presence of the target in the establishment that Taylor would exit from whichever exit, he felt was the more probable exit point of the person of interest would likely take in advance to them utilizing it. Daniel accepted his role in this play that had been forced upon him. Once he obtained confirmation on the identity of Theodore Wright, who had been sitting off in the corner of the establishment.

"Hey bartender, come here for a second if you don't mind. I have a question I'd like to ask of you.", Asked Daniel.

The bartender was stuck in a usually complicated quagmire. He was always the designated point of contact for law enforcement.

He just had to communicate with the individual without appearing to enjoy the experience. So, the bartender reluctantly approached Daniel, and Asked him if he wanted a drink.

"No, I am not thirsty at the moment.", responded Daniel

At this, the bartender attempted to make a visual display of his reluctance to serve Daniel let alone converse with him longer than he had to for the sole purpose of business for his boss. He simply started to walk back to the other end of the bar area since Daniels initial response was that he wasn't thirsty at the time. Meanwhile Taylor had already found himself a seat and was consuming his first drink from one of the mobile servers floating around. Now Daniel, recognizing what has taken place. He also understands what is required of his role. Taylor is amused watching Daniels' decisions as the scenes play itself out.

"Hello, Bartender, excuse me one more time my brother!" shouted Daniel as low as he could while still being loud enough to be heard by the bartender at the far end of the bar.

The bartender pretended that he was unable to hear Daniel for as long as he could without making a scene out of the situation. The bartender finally returned to Daniel at his location along the bar.

"Would you like something to drink now", The bartender made his position clear with medium volume.

"Yes, I will have rum and coke. And also, can you please tell me who that individual sitting across from the jukebox is? I am grateful for any information you may have to share with me Brother." Daniel retorted in a low enough tone to be difficult to ease drop and hear as he slipped the bartender a hundred-dollar bill.

"Ok, let me get you your drink Brother." Said the bartender.

As the bartender returned to his register... putting the hundred dollar bill into the air to pretend to examine its authenticity as he travelled. This maneuver made the majority of the customers in the establishment uneasy because it was a clear signal that the money was in exchange for information about someone in the joint or someone that was known to patronize the joint. Nether was an acceptable concept. Since Daniel's ocular device had been synchronized with the entire team everyone could see on their individual displays the verification of the target in the establishment. When the bartender had returned with Daniels' drink, Daniel raised the glass to his face and commenced to drink a long swig. It was at this moment that Theodore made his move to exit from the rear door. Taylor then went to the restroom which was also in the rear of the bar. Daniel rushed out the front, leaving the rest of his drink behind. Taylor took his time making his way to the bathroom. Once he got beyond where he could be seen by the other patrons, he also utilized the back door to gain entry to the path behind the establishment to the side street.

Once outside, Taylor instructed team leader six to send the tracking information on Theodore to his ocular device, so he could maintain a reasonable distance to the target without causing him to do anything drastic from feeling followed or pinned down. The system was able to do so after his heat signature had been captured by the thermal imager utilized within the acquired satellite package. With that, his position was monitored via display within Team Six's vehicle amongst other Op related data such as coordinated communication with the Closed-circuit television monitoring services for the regional municipalities. His location tracked his whereabouts and sent visual tracking information to the ocular devices of the team members in pursuit.

His position was currently moving quickly across Seventh Street towards the Arena next door. Team Three and Four had already converged on his location, Team leader and two members of her team jumped out of their vehicle, discreetly applied two electrified Taser prongs to his front and rear chest cavity area. Upon his loss of consciousness from the electricity dispensed, his limp body was quickly picked up and carried into their vehicle with deceptive discretion. The whole scene had been dispersed within ten to fifteen seconds.

took him into custody. The convoy began its departure back to the building.

"Good job Team." Exclaimed Daniel over their connected communication devices. He even had to smile in Taylor's direction.

CHAPTER II

"Puzzle Piece"

The Convoy had made it back to the building with Theodore and Efren. Efren had been an occupant of team one's vehicle the entirety of the trip. Efren confirmed the identification of Theodore after he was taken into custody once he had been tased. As the teams began to exit their vehicles on the parking deck, an additional member of Demetrius' special service team rushed out to them with a wheelchair for Theodore, since he was still slightly unconscious. Efren was taken back to the conference room where Ronald was still being held. Theodore was beginning to wake up as he was being rolled along amongst the entourage of security professionals.

As he was attempting to readjust his eyes to the brightness of the lights within the conference room, what he did realize was that he recognized Ronald and Efren sitting across from him at the conference table. This brought him to great anger and belligerence.

"Both of you are some ungrateful ass snitch-made bitches!", scowled Theodore as he elongated his annunciation of his last word.

Ronald and Efren both at that just looked off with moderate embarrassment. As that reunion was just starting to warm up, Demetrius was in an adjacent room when he was notified by Arthur that Khaleel and Vaughn had pulled up to the building with two vehicle loads of men requesting access into the parking structure. They wanted to see him and they also wanted to visit Langston as well. Demetrius gave Arthur permission to let them through. Their Vehicles reached the level of the parking deck where Demetrius, Taylor and Daniel had been waiting for them. The three of them were in discussion as to their approach to the pending interrogation that was soon to begin.

"Well, this just got more interesting. My Uncle Khaleel will not be in the best of dispositions as it is. If I was to share with him that it was in the pursuit of these three men, is how Langston got injured more or less his attention will shift his disgruntled aggression towards them. This will without question enhance our abilities in obtaining the timey information we need right now. And we won't be deviating that far from the truth in doing so. Just tweaking some of the information. Just a bit.", Taylor propositioned the men.

Demetrius looked over to Taylor with a mischievous smirk and nodded his head up and down before speaking.

"Sounds good to me. I spoke to Khaleel a few hours ago. Seems like he had already spoken to Vaughn and he definitely wasn't very pleased with how things took place. Amongst other things we discussed the subject at some length.", responded Demetrius.

The men then all nodded in agreement as Khaleel's vehicles pulled into the spaces right in front of where they had been standing. Almost simultaneously all the vehicle doors burst open, and the occupants of both vehicles departed from within the heavy thumping, based music, coming from inside each vehicle. The music was briefly increasingly deafening as the doors were slung open. Soon after the doors opened, and the group exited both trucks, the ignitions were cut off, and the music stopped. There then stood Khaleel, Vaughn, Manny, and quite a few more men standing behind Khaleel who was standing in front of Demetrius.

"It's been a minute Brother. We definitely need to do better. I understand that my nephew is somewhere in your fortress unconscious?" Khaleel announced.

"Yeah, Langston is being cared for round the clock. My nephew is beginning to show positive signs of recuperation. You won't be stopped by me in seeing him, just respect that he is convalescing and will need the least amount of disturbance so he can rest and recover as soon as possible. But before you go and see him, I need you coincidentally enough to assist us in dealing with some of the issues surrounding his incident. He was with Denard and Taylor searching for three men. These men are suspects in the disappearances of over twenty women in this community. Our community. We wanted to grab them and bring them back here to get information from them. Time is not on our side in this. You and the influence of your team can expedite this process. Or so I believe it can anyway." Responded Demetrius.

"Am I supposed to know these men D? Seems like you already know the answer to that. Now comes the part where you skip past the Inception shit and get real with me... Time isn't on my side either. I got shit to handle. I'm only here to check up on Langston. From fuckin' with you and ya brother. Ya brother who aint even here right now...So cut to it family." barked Khaleel back at Demetrius.

"Fair enough Kha. Fair enough. You know I have access to a lot of information. This one guy Ronald Evans, He moves products for Manny off around Minnesota. He rolls with another fella named Efren. Both of them were approached by this last one to arrange to have their previous girlfriends kidnapped and the information from them as to the most opportune time to do such a thing for a few grand a piece. We need you to utilize your reverence in the community to encourage a very fruitful dump of information on hopefully where any of these women are, who has them, and anything else that we can use to get the women back tonight. It goes without saying that the more information we can uncover about the group that pulled all of this off in our backyard will assist all of us in preventing it from happening again, or sending a very loud message on the Hill as well as in these streets that nobody best not try to do it again. How was that? Better?", Demetrius smugly retorted.

Khaleel took a moment to digest Demetrius's proposition in addition to the information he had shared about the individuals he had detained. Manny tapped Khaleel on his hip and then leaned into his ear as he whispered to him.

"I know that Ronald guy. He does work for us K. He will not be a problem for me to get any-thing out of him. You just say the word.

He is definitely going to shit his pants when he sees either of us. Now that Theodore guy. I know him too. He won't be any problem either boss. not at all. Say the word. I'm on that, really quick too."

Demetrius stood waiting for a response from Khaleel. So did Taylor. Khaleel took an additional moment as he thought quickly looking in the direction of the doorway leading out of the parking area to inside the building...

"Let's Go. Manny bring your guys with me. The rest of you hold up here until I call for you. Once we get done with this, we're going to pay Langston a visit then we go out. Nothing has changed, we still have shit to do. moves to make. Stay Ready." Commanded Khaleel.

At that the group of men; Daniel, Taylor, Demetrius, Khaleel, Manny and about four others grimly looking individuals started to walk hesitantly into the building. During this time Theodore was still laying into both Ronald and Efren, more so Ronald. Expletive after expletive. Insult after insult, and threat after threat. For the most part Ronald and Efren were unmoved by all this. Largely in part from having a building thrown on top of them and surviving due to the rigidity of the men detaining them. Witnessing the political power of their hosts in having law enforcement and the military escort them out. After riding some military grade miniature barge system across the Potomac... Plus Ronald was aware and made Efren aware that eventually he had a distinct feeling that his boss Manny would find his way to them since he knew Taylor had strong connections to Manny and the guy, they all worked for.... So, they just sat there and absorbed whatever Theodore had to say. They knew he wasn't going to get to physically get close enough to either of them to execute any of his threats so they just waited. Eventually this unexpectedly odd reaction to his usual aggressive demeanor had even begun to wear away at Theodore's comfortability of rambling and carrying on with his threatening overtures.

Then the conference door busted open. In came an unpleasant, and displeased Khaleel, a wound-up Manny, and four goons of peak physical fitness rushing the room, wasting no time whatsoever in grabbing up a completely astonished and panicked Theodore up out of his seat. He was hoisted high into the air by the largest of the goons, then abruptly smashed down into the glass conference table by chokeslam. Theodore was successfully smashed through the glass table. It was thoroughly broken into several thousand shards of glass around and beneath him in an instant. With the hand clenched increasingly tighter around the throat of the previously talkative Theodore, Manny leaned in and over Theodore's face extremely close and somewhat whispered to

Theodore...

"We definitely don't have the time today to play no games with you shit head. You know me and what I am. Unless you want to be what gets fed to my dogs, you're going to get ya fuckin' mind right and tell me and these men here every mutha-fuckin thing we ask of you. If I even think..."

Manny was interrupted by the Goon now placing both hands around his throat for better grip as he began to bounce Theodore's head aggressively off the floor that was now covered in broken glass.

"Hey! Hey! Hey!", quickly yelled Manny.

"I still need this guy Loco, if he fucks up you can finish him. Until then Let's see what he decides to do. Talk or Nah?" Manny ominously said to Theodore as he backed away from him.

At the same time the larger goon Loco also had released his grip from around his throat leaving behind a largely recognizable whelp around his neck line. As he was starting to regain the freedom from asphyxiation and ability to breathe once again, his ability to see clearly also had begun to return from him. The first images he could clearly make out where the disturbed look of both fear and angst Ronald and Efren both looked on as he was coming around from being beaten and broken so viciously and so quickly. Their collective dred brought a sharpened sense of alertness to Theodore. That and he knew exactly what Manny was. A monster who has been trying to evolve into a gargantuan monster everyday he'd ever known him. In regards to his business, Manny cared only about making sure Khaleel was satisfied with the results of his endeavors. He grew increasingly more frightened knowing that he knew these things about Manny, while realizing he had just asked him to speak on whatever he was asked and he hasn't responded yet. He was also aware of Manny's illicit reputation for a severe lack of having any resemblance to patients whatsoever.

As Theodore attempted to get himself up off of the floor and lean up against the base of the wall behind where he was just previously sitting, he was again abused and thrown into the approximate location he was trying to struggle to inch into.

Manny, beginning to haunt all three of the detainees with his pacing about slowly, as he fondled his hands and fists as he thought aloud what he desired to do next. Daniel, still shocked by what he had just seen, but not amazed took that opportunity to get right to it with his questioning...

"Theodore? Can you hear me? Can you Understand I am speaking to you?", Daniel inquired. Still curious if he had been seriously concussed in the mealy.

To this Theodore look up and over to where Daniel had been standing and squinted a bit before responding back,

"Yes, I hear you and I understand you. What the fuck do you want from me!", yelled Theodore to Daniel.

When Manny heard Theodore's voice being raised towards Daniel, he took it as a personal insult. He looked at two of his goons with wide open eyes and shook his head in disbelief. Nothing more needed to be done. Both Goons swept in and were ready to grab Theodore again. One had pulled out a blackjack on their way to where he had been laying up against the wall. Daniel intervened however,

"Whoa! WHoa! Whoa now! I'm sure he is just frustrated. He did answer me. I am good with that for now. Let me finish with him. Then, if he fucks up that opportunity then you can do what you want with him. But I believe he can still help me. I want to give him that chance to do so. So, Theo, will you start by telling me Who was you getting the money from that you gave the two of these guys here [gesturing towards Efren and Ronald]. I need to know this now. I want to be able to find these people today Theo. You can really save us all a great deal of time by telling me where I can find; Claudine Miller, Alissa Rodriguez, Noreen Martin, Merita Delgado, Paige Jackson, and any other women taken by these people in the area. What will you tell me about these women Theo...?", Daniel asked.

Before Theodore could look up and respond, one of Manny's Goons swooped in and cold clocked Theodore across the chin. He quickly slumped over in the opposite direction of the punch. Before he was completely slumped to the opposite side Manny swooped in from the other side and slapped the shit out of him. So much so that it woke him backup and he was so shocked in the process he took a loud sharp gasp for air like he had just woken up from a bad nightmare.

"Aaaagh! [Choking very hard], There are a group of buildings, not all of them are side by side. [gasping for more air as he tries to blurt out as much as he could to avoid another beating], In the basements of these buildings located along Seamon Avenue, by Middle Branch Park, on the south end of the Hanover Street Bridge. In the Cherry Hill section of South Baltimore. There are over thirty women being held there. This is where.", Exclaimed Theodore as he was desperately trying to breathe and speak almost at the same time.

Manny, disappointed in his forthright-fullness, simply mashed him by the face back to the ground. He then stood all the way up from his kneeling position, gestured to two of his goons, Daniel and Taylor for them to leave. He left two of his goons behind with Khaleel and instructed them,

"If We get up there and find out that it was a trap and this piece of shit wasted even more of my time. I want you to take him to the warehouse and cut off his dick. Then I want you to cut off fingers and toes every twenty minutes after. When I return, I will do far worse to him for this..."

They exited what was left of Demetrius conference room immediately after Manny finished speaking. Khaleel left after, leaving the room with Ronald, Efren and what remained of Theodore. One of the goons Zip tied Theodores hands together, then did the same for his feet. After that he did the same to both Efren and Ronald. Once this was complete Khaleel departed the room too. Khaleel, upon entering the hallway met with Demetrius, and they Shook hands in agreement that it seemingly went well pending the information being verified. The both of them then started to make their way towards the area of the building where Colin was being watched over by his medical staff.

"I just need to make two calls Bro. We can walk as I do that... on our way up to the elevator. I'm not having conversations... just getting the ball rolling on what those guys are following up on in Baltimore.", Demetrius said.

"No Problem. We have quite a bit of time. I plan to stick around if you don't mind... [as he lightly chuckled], and see this thang through.", Khaleel answered back.

So, Demetrius grabbed a mobile device from the interior pocket of his sports jacket and began to dial out.

"Hello, Stuart? [inaudible] ..., Hey it's me Delegate Fortune. I may need your support on a local matter that has seemed to reach your neck of the woods. We can discuss the details a little later. I have two teams enroute to South Baltimore to conduct a lastminute investigative work based on some information I just had dropped on my lap regarding some human trafficking wave gotten wind to in the area. [inaudible] ... Great! I will call you back shortly."

Demetrius pressed a button, and ended the call. Then just as he did before, he dialed a second number out, and waited for the recipient of his call to pick up the line.

"Yes, may I speak to Madam Present Wilson? [Inaudible] ... Yes, Hello Diane. I just got off the line with Stuart. We covered the basic situation and I was hoping you could be free later this evening for a somewhat quick conference call. We can possibly wrap things up and recieved some recognition for putting a dent in a human trafficking cell in our collective areas of

accountabilities... [Inaudible] ... So yes, that along the lines of what I had in mind. Speak to you soon. I will call you first so you can get Barry in on the call as well. He will feel better knowing that you brought him in on the call.", Demetrius put the mobile device back into his coat pocket.

As both men approached the elevator lobby, Demetrius apologized for the need to make his calls and thanked Khaleel for his patience. The doors to the elevator opened simultaneous to Demetrius pressing the button to summon the car. As the two men entered the car, they began to converse in Langston condition. Meanwhile Taylor, Daniel and Manny and company were approaching their destination. They were also accompanied by an additional five vehicles. These additional vehicles were a special unit dispatched by Demetrius to serve as backup in case things became untenable. With a few minutes to spare before Taylor and company had reached their exit, Taylor and Daniel reinitiated their network and synchronized their ocular devices. Manny did not have any ocular device so he sat and watched the two of them with moderate bewilderment.

Taylor was aware of the support team dispatched by his uncle.

Demetrius had sent him a text message informing him of doing so.

He also sent a link through the text message that enabled Taylor to sync up with their network as well. In doing so, Taylor also synced up Daniel with them as well. These were members of Demetrius special security force just as Daniel was so they were already familiar with each other. Daniel, once synced up on his comm link began to issue instructions to the support units,

"Units one thru three, Take the 'Waterview Avenue with the rest of us, and proceed straight on that route. Establish a watch perimeter between the Waterview Ave side of the Baltimore Rowing Club House and the Seven Eleven store at the intersection of Waterview Ave and Potee Street/ Hwy two. Unit four, Follow the lead vehicles when we take the same Waterview Exit of the twoninety-five onto Waterview Ave as well. from there we will all turn right onto Cherry Hill Road. The lead vehicles will then continue on Cherry Hill Road until we make the right on Ronald Road. We will wait close to that intersection for the rest of the team to get into position. Unit Four, continue down Cherry Hill Road until you arrive at the intersection of Cherry Land Road and Cherry Hill Road. Continue by making the left onto Cherry Hill Road. Make the next left onto Seabury Road and hold position near the intersection discreetly. Unit Five continues after Unit Four makes the left onto Seabury Road and then makes a left at the intersection of Cherry Hill Road and Seamon Avenue. Hold position right before the approaching the westward curve. On my call the lead vehicles will engage the target location."

Then oddly enough Taylor, having learned a few things from his outing with his father recently, and what transpired that evening, decided to instruct his ocular device to analyze the area they had intended to approach more scrutinous. Taylor then advised Daniel.

"Get the Satellite package up and running before we move into the go position, and run a thermal analysis of every building on Seamon Avenue within the target area. Think clearly, we will find opposition here without question, so let's get a jump on identifying just what type of opposition we will find. Better yet what awaits us."

When the package came online, even Manny was somewhat taken aback when the imagery came back revealing that there were more than thirty well-armed men spread across the string of basement dwellings, more than fifty women huddled in corners in rooms fortified by the men guarding the basements. With this, Daniel restructured his teams.

"Teams One through Three leave one behind and arm the vehicle defensive array. Maneuver through the tree line to the rear of the buildings snake in some cams and give us a closer look at where they are positioned within the basements."

"Lead Units, with me. We will engage from the front, enter the buildings and proceed to their basement areas. Since our targets are below ground, we will secure and maintain the high ground by keeping them fox holed in. Lead Unit two, maintain thermal imagery. Pick off every aggressor as they emerge. Top priority on getting past them to the imprisoned women. When you bag one, get a snapshot of anybody ink you can find on them before moving forward."

Taylor and the two men that came with Many started to exit the vehicle at the top of the west end of Seamon. As they approached the first building Taylor initiated the thermal feature in his ocular device. He stopped the group with him and communicated to

Daniel to dispatch that he could see about five M.A.M. groups [Military aged males] in the main lobby of the building he was outside.

"Weapons silent everyone. Paint each building for target M.A.M. gatherings Lead two... Once we light up building one, we may be able to draw a group of them to reinforce their teams in building one. If this happens, we can send units one through three to double back and rescue the women in the least occupied building first. Get them back through the tree line. I will get a van enroute now."

Taylor, Manny and his two approached building one. Taylor and Manny's goons Took out the first two as planned and exchanged fire with the last three as expected. Also as expected, the gunfire drew most of the men from the other buildings out from their underground positions to reinforce the first building Tylor and

Manny had hit. As they emerged out of the other buildings, Team Four and Five were quickly picking them off while maintaining their cover amongst the darkness. It wasn't long before there weren't many more coming out of the buildings. According to the unit observing the Thermal coverage,

"Lead two to Team Leader."

"Team Leader go." responded Daniel,

"We are down to less than ten identified M.A.M.'s. Unit One, Two and Three have cleared and secured women from four buildings in the process. So far totaling over thirty-six women accounted for and past the tree line Sir. There are still seventeen women spread between two remaining buildings. Seems like we were lucky enough and caught them off guard. From what I can see off the satellite display there is much confusion amongst the remaining M.A.M.'s within visual."

"Before long we will have law enforcement on the scene. We know Delegate Fortune if he hasn't already done so he is probably in the process of establishing contact with the necessary officials here in B'more to cover our six. So, the less combatant teams we leave to speak the better. It will be our story to tell when the time comes. These women snatching sons of bitches don't get no mercy no how. matter of fact. I have just the thing.", Daniel suddenly ceased his communication, then caught himself and began once more.

"Walter! Grab the hush puppy out the truck." Daniel gleefully shouted.

Manny, his team and Taylor looked at one another astonishingly in bewilderment trying to figure out what the hush puppy could have been but something to laugh at. When Walter came back to their position holding a bag of oblong shaped frag grenade looking devices. Their curiosity grew exponentially.

"Marcellus had been developing these for the past few years now with Demetrius's lab back in DC. They are a prototype variant of a chloroform gas that is weak enough to moderately incapacitate the enemy long enough for us to Get the drop and take a significant first strike in close quarter combat. Let's throw a few of these in the basement in the direction of where the remaining M.A.M.

teams were, then go in heavy. It will definitely quicken things up." Said Walter, as he sensed the need to calm their confusion.

Manny went with his two and some of Daniel's men to do just what Daniel planned and Walter explained in the second to last building to be addressed. Taylor, Daniel and a few of Daniels' other team members stuck together and approached the first of the two buildings left to address. They coordinated their entries. Before the remaining identified M.A.M.'s knew what hit them, they were all taken down with precision. Manny and his team took the job of Collecting photos of the tattoos worn by each man down. As this transpired local PD arrived on the scene. Already contacted by the Mayor, they were arriving in a support capacity.

They also collected the deceased and sent their fleet of coroners' vehicles full of the group of dead traffickers back down to DC so their carcasses could be more thoroughly vetted for identifiable markings. Manny and his goons were not so appreciative of having wasted their time hustling to account for the images they had already collected, as they moved quickly to get as much as

possible before BPD arrived. Not knowing they weren't going to have to make a run for it. Manny was definitely not accustomed to not having Law to contend with. An ambulance arrived and evaluated each of the rescued women. Once that brief triage had concluded they too were sent off in a comfortable stream of coach buses, back to DC for identification and further evaluation.

Daniel went off with his team and briefly communicated with the support Units from BPD. Whereas, Taylor, Manny, and his goons went back to the truck and was preparing for the trip home.

Taylor took a moment to get some separation and contact his Uncle. Taylor pulled a mobile device from one of his many pockets and pressed a few buttons.

"It's good to hear your voice, nephew. What's your status?", inquired Demetrius

"We got the job done Uncle D. That shit was dope too. How is

Langston? I feel a lot better now that his sacrifice wasn't in vain. Now we just need for him to pull through. How's he doing?", was Taylor's response.

"Langston is stable and improving from what my Med staff has indicated. How many women were rescued? were any of them killed or injured in the process?", asked Demetrius.

"From what I know at the moment, none that I am aware of. We got them all out safe. There were fifty-four women in total. It was insane to see this was happening right underneath all of us. This trafficking thing is alarming and real. I have a strong feeling that we will not like what we find in regards to who these men were, or more importantly, who they worked for. By the way BPD as you most likely know are enroute to your cadaver lab with over thirty carcasses. We caught these assholes with their pants down. I have a strong feeling they were on the verge of transporting these women soon. We are on our way back down."

"That's fantastic Nephew! I know that feeling well. All of y'all did an amazing job last minute and were short noticed. There is unfortunately way more women and even children getting abducted every day. It is insane when you actually think about that shit. Well, we did good today. That's what counts for right now. I'll be waiting for all of you when you get back. The lab is already set up and ready to get this process of identifying begun."

Taylor thought long and hard on the trip back to his Uncle's building about Langston, His Father, and oddly enough he thought a great deal about his Mother. He wasn't sure exactly what was in store for him on this journey, but after this episode, He felt reassured in how powerful the energy of making an actual difference in these ways was electrifying.